THE MEAN STREETS

THE "MAC" SERIES

Draw the Curtain Close (1947)
Every Bet's a Sure Thing (1953)
The Case of the Murdered Model (1954, aka *Prey for Me*)
The Mean Streets (1954)
The Brave, Bad Girls (1956)
You've Got Him Cold (1958)
The Case of the Chased and the Chaste (1959)
How Hard to Kill (1962)
A Sad Song Singing (1963)
Don't Cry for Long (1964)
Portrait of a Dead Heiress (1965)
Deadline (1966)
Death and Taxes (1967)
The King Killers (1968, aka *Death Turns Right*)
The Love-Death Thing (1969)
The Taurus Trip (1970)

THE PETE SCHOEFIELD SERIES:

And When She Stops (1957 aka *I.O.U. Murder*)
Go To Sleep, Jeannie (1959)
Too Hot For Hawaii (1960)
The Golden Hooligan (1961, aka *Mexican Slayride*)
Go, Honeylou (1962)
The Girl with the Sweet Plump Knees (1963)
The Girl in the Punchbowl (1964)
Only on Tuesdays (1964)
Nude in Nevada (1965)

THE MEAN STREETS

THOMAS B. DEWEY

WILDSIDE PRESS

TO MY WIFE
who kept this going when it appeared—
more than once—that it had come to a full and final stop.

…But down these mean streets a man must go who is not himself mean—who is neither tarnished nor afraid…"

—Raymond Chandler

CHAPTER ONE

He came tearing down the street with this newspaper in his hand, looking back over his shoulder, and I figured he'd swiped it from some stand. I moved to get out of his way, but he looked around suddenly and swerved toward me, the way it sometimes happens. Then he banged into me, grabbing at my coat, and I got hold of one of his arms and steadied him. He looked at me quick and hard and, still holding the paper, backed away panting and leaned against the iron fence that bordered the sidewalk.

He was eight years old, maybe nine. His face was dirty, his eyes sharp, and his chin stuck out far enough to prove he wasn't scared of nothing in this world—that he knew about.

He might have been myself, looking back at me over thirty years. Plenty of it was the same: the scarred, twisted fence he slouched against, gripping the paper; the dirty, crowded street, lined with battered trash cans and behind them the leaning tenements with the broken steps and nothing but cement between the bottom step and the leaning firetrap across the way; the strident yells, the raucous traffic—plenty the same.

Only it was a different street, in a different city, and this kid would have a different name. Also, the cars were later models, there weren't any horses mixed in with them, and if these changes didn't amount to anything, I had changed myself—some.

"Big hurry," I said, grinning at him.

He didn't grin back. He didn't say anything. He just stared at me, catching his breath, and after a few seconds, he began to edge away along the fence, with that paper clutched in one hand.

"Maybe you could tell me," I said, trying to hold him, "I'm looking for Arvin's place—" His eyes widened in spite of himself.

"Louis Arvin?" he said.

"No. Joey."

"Oh. Louis's brudda."

"Louis's brudda. You know where he lives?"

"Yeh."

"I'm from the high school."

The eyes narrowed again.

"Hooky cop?"

"No. I'm the baseball coach."

"Oh," he said. "You the new guy—"

"I'm the new guy."

He was holding the paper, folded tightly, along one thigh and he shifted it now to his other hand, glanced down at it, then both ways along the fence.

"Could you tell me where Joey lives?" I tried again.

He started to point with the paper, then checked himself and used his free hand.

"Down there. Three places. Third floor."

"Thanks," I said. "What's your name?"

He looked down at his feet.

"Spig," he said.

"All right, Spig. Thanks again. Could I have my wallet back now?"

His eyes jerked up at me, then fell. He looked at the paper and along the fence, as if he might try to make a break. Then slowly, reluctantly, he opened the paper, reached into one of the folds and came up with my wallet. It took him a while longer to get it out where I could reach it. I held it in my hand, looking at him, while he lifted one bare foot and scratched the bottom of it along his other leg.

What do you do now, Mac? I thought. Shake your finger? Tell him he's a bad boy and he should never do this again? What does a good school-teacher do in a case like this? What happened to yourself the first time? The guy slugged you in the side of the head and you bled from the ear all night. So the next time, you figured it smarter and got away. But there was nothing in it except a couple of tickets to the Firemen's Ball.

Or talk straight across to him maybe. Look, kid, this won't get you any place. Cut it out. A good, solid line: Crime doesn't pay. Of course, in Spig's world, nothing else pays either and there's always a chance that crime might. So maybe you better save the lecture and get on with it.

His hard voice cut across my thoughts like a saw.

"I didn't know," he said. "I didn't know who you was."

It had to be his show. I waited.

"Joey says—" he swallowed, "maybe you're O.K."

"He does?"

"He says he can't figure you. He says sometimes you're O.K. and sometimes you're a jerk."

I found a dollar bill in the wallet.

"Well, Spig," I said, holding out the buck, "let's say I'm only a part-time jerk."

He stared at the bill and I had to wave it at him before he would take it. But his tongue was licking his lips and it wasn't politeness that made him hesitate. He was trying to spot the hook.

"This is for directing me to Joey's," I said. "There were only two bucks in the thing anyway. We split fifty-fifty. That fair?"

He looked at his feet, snagged the bill with his thin fingers and stuck it in a pocket.

"Is Joey gonna die?" he said.

"Joey—? No. Certainly not."

He looked both ways again and got confidential.

"Louis says—Joey's brudda—that if Joey dies, he's gonna kill the punk that trun the ball."

"Louis says this?"

"Louis's tough, Mister. He just come back from doin' a stretch at the state farm."

"Joey won't die," I said, "and Louis won't kill anybody."

"He might."

"Would Campanella kill Allie Reynolds if he got hit in the head?"

"I don't know about Campanella. But Louis Arvin might kill anybody, if he felt like it—if Mr. Smith would let him."

"Mr. Smith?"

"Yeh."

"Who's Mr. Smith?"

His face closed stubbornly.

"I di'nt say nothin'."

"All right. You didn't say nothing."

"But Joey better not die."

"He won't die."

He did a funny little shuffle with both feet, then broke suddenly and ran off along the fence. I watched him to the corner. He stood there a minute, casing the immediate area, then threw the paper down and walked out of sight.

Sixty million guys, I thought, in between and on both sides of Roy Campanella and Louis Arvin. Which one will you be, Spig, when you grow up? If you grow up.

Now you're being a jerk, I thought then, a full-time jerk. Get on with the business. What if Joey should die? He won't. But he certainly got hit awfully hard in the head by that ball and it took him a couple of hours to come out of it. And he hasn't come back to school yet, after three days. And a small-time big shot, Louis Arvin, waiting for him to die...

I walked on toward the row of tenements ahead. The iron fence enclosed a vacant lot strewn with rubbish and came to an end at an alley midway along the block. There was a cigar store with a soda fountain just beyond the alley and then the tenements began. A couple of punks were loafing in front of the store. I didn't pay any attention to them. It was four-thirty in the afternoon and those of the neighborhood who worked were straggling home, driving old, dented cars—once in a while a new one—or walking with a dreary shuffle. There were some women on the street, loaded with shopping bags or pushing bedraggled baby carriages, or just sitting on the steps of the buildings. I had seen it all before, in different places, but always the same. Only the names had been changed.

I thought about it, climbing the three flights of rickety stairs in Joey's building. You can change the names and faces, the numbers, the geographical location. But you can't change the smell. The smell remains— the same complex smell of stale food, dirt, soot and human flesh, also dog and cat, and leaking gas jets, all blended in one huge aroma that you had got used to once, had got away from and unused to and kept running into again and again. So you could set me down, blindfolded, in the midst of that aroma and I could give you all the statistics; a description of the buildings, the streets, the people and the dogs and cats and it would all fit, give or take a statistic here or there. So maybe part of what drove Spig to snatch my wallet was the smell. Maybe you had to try to get from a world that stank to a world that smelled good. There had to be such a world. Didn't there?

I knocked on the door of Number 36, where a white card had been thumbtacked to the scratched panel. The card bore the name Arvin, printed neatly in pencil. I knocked again and a third time and the door opened three inches. A woman of twenty-five or thirty looked through the crack at me. She was wearing a chenille bathrobe, holding the lapels tight together across her chest. She didn't say anything, just looked, and after a while I cleared my throat and said, "I'm a part-time jerk, come to see about Joey Arvin."

It threw her off just enough to keep her from slamming the door in my face.

"Joey's asleep," she said. "Some other time."

Then she had rallied and was closing the door. I put a hand on it.

"Please," I said, "just a second—I'm from the school."

Resentment flared like torches in her eyes.

"If you're coming to drag Joey back—"

"No. I'm the coach. I just wanted to see how he is."

"Not now!"

From somewhere inside came another voice—Joey's.

"Who is it, Francie?"

She looked back over her shoulder, then at me again through the crack in the door.

"I won't stay long," I said. "I won't get him upset."

She wavered, but she wouldn't open the door. Joey's voice came again, louder this time.

"Francie! Who is it? Is it Louis?"

She yelled back at him.

"No! It's the guy from school. The coach."

Joey said something else, but I couldn't make out the words. I saw the girl's chenille-covered shoulder shrug slightly and the door swung open.

"Come on in," she said, "but make it fast. I'm dressing. I got to go to work."

"Thanks, Francie." I stepped into the room. "You're Joey's sister?"

She slammed the door shut and walked away from me across the dingy room.

"I'm his sister, mother, father and all his uncles and aunts," she said. "He's in here."

She was quite a pretty girl, with black, thick hair, down now around her shoulders, and though I couldn't tell much with that robe around her, it was clear that her figure was firm and good. With any luck, she might still get away, before the smell and the dirt and the Louis Arvins and the cigar store punks made a shapeless nobody out of her.

Then I got my mind into other channels as we walked into a small bedroom opposite the door, where Joey Arvin was propped up in bed with a bandage over one side of his head and his left eye still badly swollen.

CHAPTER TWO

I stood there a minute, looking at Joey; then the sister went on through another door and closed it, and I heard water running in the bathroom. Joey hadn't said anything.

"What happened?" I said. "You run into a horse or something?"

He grinned feebly.

There was a chair near the bed with some movie magazines piled on it.

"Would it be all right if I sat down?"

"Yeh—sure," Joey said. "Sit down."

I pushed the magazines to the back of the chair and sat down on the edge of it.

"How do you feel?" I asked him.

He shrugged, wincing at the movement.

"O.K.," he said.

"I feel kind of funny about it. I talked you into coming out for the team, and what happens? You get hit in the head with a ball."

"Ah-h—" he said vaguely, shrugging again.

"Denton feels bad about it. He asked me to find out whether he could get anything for you."

"I guess not."

Bill Denton was the pitcher who had thrown the wild ball. He was from another environment, a good, clean kid—but then, I checked my thoughts, they were both good, clean kids—so far.

What is a good, clean kid? I wondered.

"That looks like the same bandage we put on at school," I said. "Haven't you had a doctor?"

"Nah. What do I want with a doctor?"

"With something in the head like that, it's a good idea—"

"I don't want no doctor!"

"All right, Joey."

He was a little embarrassed to have yelled at me and he turned his head away and looked at the wall. Pretty soon he said, "There's a game tomorrow."

"That's right."

"Will we win it?"

I let some time go by.

"It will be tough without you, Joey," I said, "but we'll try."

"I guess it don't matter much."

"In a way, it doesn't. But it would be nice to win it."

"Will—Denton be pitching?"

"I think so."

His lips tightened. I couldn't tell whether it was with anger or regret that he wouldn't be in the game.

"I guess I won't be able to come out no more."

"Wouldn't want you to try it this season, Joey. Takes time to get over these things. Maybe next year—"

"I mean—Francie says I got to get a job. I wasn't supposed to come out anyway."

"Guy can't work all the time, Joey."

"I got to make a little money. Francie works too hard. And there's not only me—there's Louis."

"Louis doesn't have a job?"

"Louis? Louis never had a job!" He said it proudly. "Louis was doing time for the last two years." That he said less proudly, but firmly and without hesitation.

"I heard," I said.

"Louis's smart. He'll think of something."

I let that pass. After a while he said, slowly, tentatively, as from a distance, "I—might not go back to school next year."

"Not go back?"

He flared again. The anger was always just under the surface. When it would break, you could see it coming behind his eyes and in the set of his jaw.

"There's no law says I have to graduate from high school. There's only a law says you got to go till you're seventeen."

"I know what the law says. But you only have one more year to go—"

"They'll probably fail me anyway, for being out so long."

"Only three days, Joey."

"But I don't think I'll be going back. I got to make some money. Louis will find something for me. He promised."

"So he'll have two people to take care of him instead of one?"

I could have bitten off my tongue. Joey stiffened in the bed and his eyes narrowed to slits. If it hurt his head, he either didn't notice or didn't care.

"Louis's O.K., see," he said. "Louis's smart. He's my brother and he knows the score. No lousy schoolteacher can come around knockin' Louis

13

—" I went to the bed, put one hand on his shoulder and tried to ease him back down.

"O.K., Joey, O.K.," I said. "I'm sorry. Take it easy."

He shrugged off my hand and sank back against the pillows. He was still glaring at me, but it didn't come off too well with that bad left eye.

"Nobody can talk about Louis to me—"

"All right, Joey. Forget I said it."

There was a knock on the front door. I glanced toward the bathroom. The water was still running. Joey started to get up and I patted him down again.

"I'll go," I said.

I crossed the room and opened the door. On the other side of it stood Joey's girl, Stella Perino. She stepped back startled when she saw me, then said, "Hello, Mr. Donnelly. Is Joey here?"

"Yes. Come in."

She walked in, giving me the full benefit of her provocative, hip-twitching stride, blinking her lashes at me, smiling with her moist, red mouth. A full-fledged, sultry siren at age seventeen. And underneath, so truly beautiful, so healthy—even she couldn't manage to hide it. I had never met her, but I had seen her at the ball games and sitting around in the bleachers during practice; seen her waiting for Joey at the door of the gym and the two of them walking away together after he'd come out.

She was on her way to Joey's room when she stopped and looked back. "How is Joey?" she asked.

"I don't know. He says he's all right. I think he ought to have a doctor."

"So do I."

I couldn't tell whether she meant it or whether she was just playing up to teacher. I cursed myself for a nasty, suspicious jerk and followed her back into the bedroom.

Francie had come out, wearing the same robe, her hair damp around the edges. When I walked into the room behind Stella, she gave me a harsh look.

"You still here?" she said. "When do I get dressed?"

I glanced around. There had to be another room somewhere. Maybe brother Louis had taken it over.

"I'll be going in a minute," I said.

Stella was standing beside the bed, looking at Joey. She had a small, tissue-wrapped package in one hand.

"I saw Louis in the street," she said. "He said he'd be right up."

Joey grunted something.

"I brought you something, Joey," Stella held out the package.

"Yeah?" Joey said, reaching for it.

Francie ran to the bed and grabbed it before Joey could touch it. She turned on Stella who shrank back.

"What's in it?" Francie said. "What's in the package?"

"Please, Francie," Stella said, "it's just—"

"We'll see what's in it."

Francie began to tear at the wrappings with nervous, lacquered nails.

"No, Francie—please—" Stella pleaded.

She put a hand on Francie's arm. Francie shook her off and went on opening the package. Joey stared up at her from the bed. Stella began to cry. Francie tore the last of the tissue paper from a small white box and threw the paper on the floor. She opened the box quickly, then stood very still, looking into it. Finally she lowered her hand slowly and gave it to Joey. Joey took out the contents. It was a tie clip, a cheap one such as you might pick up at the dime store for thirty-nine cents. He held it up, looking at it.

Stella was still crying. Francie glanced at her, then looked away, tight-mouthed.

"All right," she said. "But don't let me catch you bringing in reefers or —something—like you've been known to do."

Stella had her face in her hands and said nothing.

"I'll be going, Joey," I said. "Take it easy and call me at school if you want anything."

"O.K.," he said. "Thanks, Stella."

I looked at Francie. "Could I speak to you a minute?"

She hesitated.

"A short minute," she said.

She came into the room with me and closed the bedroom door, glancing back once at Stella, who hadn't moved. When she turned to face me, her eyes were veiled and I thought she might be worried over her outburst about the reefers. But she shrugged it off in a hurry.

"Well?" she said.

"How do you think Joey really is?"

"How should I know?"

"Have you had a doctor for him?"

She laughed, a hard, bitter laugh in her throat.

"Who am I?" she said. "Mrs. Vanderbilt?"

"The school will send a doctor. It wouldn't cost anything."

"A doctor? Or a cop? A truant officer maybe, and some nurse that's too feeble and old to climb the stairs—"

"No, a real doctor. Why are you against it?"

"The school sent *you.* Isn't that enough?"

"I'm not a doctor."

"Then I don't owe you anything."

Not only was I not getting anywhere; I was slipping backwards. I did some shrugging myself, inspected the crease in my hat and backed toward the door.

"All right, Francie," I said. "Have it your way. But I'd like to see Joey taken care of."

She watched me to the door. Then she took a couple of steps and let me have it, full force.

"Listen, I'll tell you why I don't want the school to send a doctor. I can't take any more pushing around. When they send somebody, they start pushing. They ask questions. They say, 'Doesn't the boy have a mother?' 'Doesn't the boy have a father?' They say, 'You'll have to do this, you'll have to do that!'"

She ran her hands through her beautiful hair.

"For God's sake!" she said. "I get pushed around all the time. It's part of the job. I'm a waitress, see? In a dump, a real dump. I get pushed and poked and patted and pinched till I'm black-and-blue from here to there. I walk home from work at three-thirty in the morning—I never know whether I'll make it. You've seen the street—" The engine ran down. Whatever had held her together while she made the speech collapsed. She slumped all over as if her bones had turned to Jell-O.

"But I guess a guy like you wouldn't understand," she said. "You have to live it to really appreciate it."

A guy like me. I looked at her and I didn't feel good. Talking to me that way had brought her alive for a while. Especially in the face. She had a wonderful face and she hadn't yet begun to make it up, so you could see everything there was in it. It was a hell of a fine face and I looked into it and thought:

I hate to stand here and be a lie, Francie. I understand maybe better than you think. Because I'm not a schoolteacher at all. I'm a kind of a cop, a shamus, a private investigator. Not that you would go for that any more than for a jerk schoolteacher, even if I could tell you. I'm a spy really. I'm spying on you and on Joey and Stella, and the people who hired me say it's for your own good and I believe them. But there's no way in the big beautiful stinking world I can make you believe it.

I thought this so hard that for a while I imagined I had really spoken it and I looked to see whether it had registered with her. But I hadn't spoken it and her eyes were dull now, the life gone from her face.

"You better go," she said. "Stella said Louis was coming. He won't like to find you here."

I refrained from commenting on Louis. I had tried it once and it hadn't gone over. I doubted that it would go over any better with sister Francine.

"All right," I said. "But if you decide you'd like a doctor, please call me. Here's my home number. I'll make sure he doesn't ask too many questions."

I handed her a plain card on which I had written my name—my schoolteacher name—and address and phone number. She held out her hand blindly and took it.

"I'm sorry," I said, "if I've held you up. I hope things go all right."

"Forget it."

The door opened behind me and I ducked out of the way automatically. Francie caught her breath, then let it out slowly as a guy came in, kicking the door shut behind him. He got halfway across the room before he wheeled and stared at me.

"Hello, Louis," Francie said.

There was nothing hard to understand about Louis. They are six for a nickel, guys like him, in every city. You see them in the poolrooms, hanging around the cigar stores, in the cheaper bars. They hang around from the time they're sixteen, taking orders from the bigger ones, giving orders to the smaller ones, picking up a little cash here and a little there, and then they get up some nerve and steal a car or something and whether they get caught or not, they get to be big shots in that neighborhood. As a matter of fact, if they get caught and do some time, they're bigger shots than otherwise. It's like an initiation. After a stretch, they're eligible to sit in with some of the older ones and they accumulate more smaller ones to whom they can give orders. They're easy to place. Except for minor differences, they even look alike. Sharply-cut suits, expensive shoes, professional shaves, even manicures. They smell of cologne. They sometimes pass as dynamic junior executives and the best of them turn out to be successful con men. But most of them give themselves away by a nervousness in the eyes and hands which is an occupational disease with them. They are not "bad" men, any more than dynamic junior executives are necessarily "good" men. They are just very sick men and they stay sick because there is no provision in our society for making them well, but only for making them sicker.

Louis Arvin was one of them. Built slender in the hips and muscular in the shoulders, like his kid brother Joey, he stood there in the middle of the room, leaning forward a little, looking at me, then at Francie.

"Who?" he said.

"He's from the school. He came to see about Joey."

His right hand moved restlessly across his stomach.

"What about Joey?" he said.

"Just checking up," I said. "I'll be going."

I turned to open the door and he said, "Yeah. Let me help you."

17

By the time I had the door open, he was at my shoulder. I didn't look around at him. When I started through it, he gave me a push between the shoulder blades, the rough, neck-snapping kind of push, and I stumbled into the hall, grabbed at the sagging wooden rail of the stairs and got my balance. Louis Arvin was in the doorway, watching me.

"Listen," he said, "if Joey don't come out of this, you're in trouble. You and the punk that threw the ball."

I was massaging the back of my neck and he stepped inside, pushing the door to slowly.

"Don't come back, jerk," he said.

The door closed. I had my shoulder braced to go back through it before I checked myself, turned away and started down the stairs.

I was being a schoolteacher, a mild-mannered public servant. It was part of the job. I could not be myself.

But it was myself being pushed around.

Going down the stairs, I felt as if I were crawling on my hands and knees.

CHAPTER THREE

The two zoot suits were no longer in front of the cigar store when I got back to it. I went inside and ordered a Coke at the soda fountain. It was a one-man shop and the myopic old man behind the counter took a long time to get it up for me. He was a dirty old man, with dirty gray hair that needed trimming, and when he finally got the drink made, the glass slipped in his hand, he had to grab at it and, grabbing, he stuck his thumb in it. He served it anyway.

"If you don't mind," I said, "could I have another?"

He blinked at me behind his glasses.

"You mean you want two of 'em?"

"No. Just a different one from this."

"What's wrong with this?"

I could still feel it where Louis Arvin had handled me in the back.

"Because you stuck your goddam thumb in it!" I said.

He looked at his thumb, picked up the glass and peered into it, looked at his thumb again and set the glass down on the back bar. He made me another one, keeping his thumb out of it, and I paid him. When I picked it up, he lifted the glass I'd turned down and drank it.

"Tastes all right to me," he said.

"Then good for you," I said.

A couple of cigarette customers came in and he shook his head sadly as he walked out from behind the soda counter to wait on them. I drank the Coke slowly, not tasting it, but feeling the cold and sparkle of it in my throat which had begun to burn.

At the end of the soda counter there was a curtained doorway leading to a back room. The curtains were only partly drawn and glancing between them, I saw a man at a card table, playing what might have been pinochle. He played in complete silence. He was fat and his clothes would always look messy. He had a burnt-out cigar stuck between thick lips. I could tell he had a live opponent because I could see the cards fall now and then from the other side of the table, but I couldn't see the man holding them.

When I set my glass down, a shadow loomed in the open street door, hesitated briefly and then came on in. I saw that it was Bill Denton, the kid on the team who had tossed the wild pitch at Joey Arvin. He came in slowly, glancing around, as if not sure of himself in this neighborhood. He hadn't seen me yet. He was a nice-looking kid of sixteen, with sandy, crew-cut hair, dressed in blue jeans and a sweatshirt—very fashionable at the school at this time—and with a hungry kind of look on his face; hunger not for food, but for goodwill; the old "let's get along together" look. I liked him all right. Compared with Joey Arvin, he seemed on the innocent side, but that's all right if you can get away with it. He was a hell of a good athlete, and that always helps.

When he saw me at the fountain, his face brightened up and he came right over.

"Hi, Coach," he said.

"Have a Coke," I said.

He shook his head reluctantly.

"I better not—all that sugar," he said. "I'm in training, remember?"

"Oh yeah." I remembered. "Well, have a lemonade."

The old man came back and managed to make us two unthumbed drinks and we stood there, drinking them. Bill didn't say anything till we had nearly finished.

"Did you see Joey?" he asked then.

"Yes, I saw him."

"How is he, Coach?"

"I think he'll be all right. Seems to feel pretty good. Still looks funny in the eye."

Bill looked around the room.

"I came down—I thought I'd go see him—" I stared into my glass.

"Did he ask you to come, Bill?"

"Well, no."

"You might wait a while. Give him a few more days."

"But I have to know. I have to find out—"

"Find out what?"

"Is he sore at me?"

"Nah," I said, looking at the glass.

"He doesn't think I hit him on purpose, does he? I wouldn't do that."

"Naturally. He doesn't think any such thing."

I wondered whether he did.

"Joey and I always got along swell—most of the time."

"I know."

"I thought, if I just went up for a minute, to tell him I'm sorry—something—" My fingers were tight on the glass and I forced them to relax.

"You do what you want to, Bill," I said, "but if you want my opinion, I wouldn't go up right now."

"Well, naturally, I'm glad to have your opinion."

"As a matter of fact," I went on, groping for a way to break it gently, "if I were you, I wouldn't stay in this neighborhood right now."

He didn't do any groping. He got it right away, where it hurt.

"Then he is sore at me. They're all sore at me," he said. "They think I did it on purpose. I got to go up there, Coach. I got to straighten it out with Joey."

"I'm sure you can straighten it out with Joey. But why not wait till you can see him alone?"

"He's got company now?"

"Company and family. He's pretty well tied up."

"Oh. Well, whatever you say."

He was badly troubled and he twirled the empty glass around on the wet counter with his fingers. Finally he twirled it too hard and it fell onto the floor and broke.

You'd have thought the old guy in the glasses had been shot. He stiffened, crept to the counter and leaned way out to look.

"Them glasses cost me twenty cents apiece," he said.

I took the dollar bill out of my wallet and laid it down.

"All right," I said. "He didn't do it on purpose."

Bill was upset now about the glass. He leaned down and started to pick up the pieces and I tapped his shoulder.

"Let it go," I said. "It's paid for."

"I'm sorry, Coach," he said.

"Forget it. Let's get out of here."

As I picked up my change and turned away from the counter, more shadows loomed in the door. This time, three guys came in. Two of them looked like the two punks who'd been hanging around earlier. The third was Louis Arvin. He headed for the cigar counter and I started out with Bill. But Arvin must have seen me with a corner of his eye, because he stopped suddenly, spun around and said:

"Well, if it ain't our beloved baseball coach. Or should I say 'Mister Coach'?"

I gave Bills arm a push, trying to get him going, but then Arvin was in front of me, his legs apart, his eyes dancing nervously in his head.

"Stick around and be sociable," he said. "Let me buy you a drink." He looked for the old man. "Hey, Pop! Set 'em up for the coach."

"No, thanks," I said, trying to push by. "I've got to be going."

His fingers on my arm were like steel springs.

"Stick *around*, Coach," he said. "I'm buying."

I could feel the fire now, like a thin, red wire, twisting up from way down deep. I yelled mentally at Bill Denton to get going, but he couldn't hear it. He stayed. I looked at Louis Arvin and tried to swallow some of the wire.

Give it a try, I thought, telling myself. Give it a fair trial.

"I really mean it," I said. "I've got to go. Maybe we can have a drink some other time."

I took Bill's arm firmly and we started for the door. Louis Arvin let us get by all right. Then he kicked the back of my left knee and I fell heavily against the cigar counter, rolled over quickly and came up on the other knee, looking for him. He and his two pals were lined up at the soda fountain, laughing fit to kill.

The red wire was twisting in my chest and it was only Bill Denton's presence that kept me on my knee long enough to give it another fair trial.

If you try to take the joint apart, Mac, I thought, it may get into the papers. You're not here to show Bill Denton how to beat up a hoodlum, though that might be useful information for him to have. You're here to set him a good example and, at the moment, to get him away from the neighborhood.

I rose slowly, dusting my pants at the knees.

"Ready for that drink now, teacher?" Arvin said.

He started toward me with a glass full of Coke in his hand. My hat had fallen off when I went down and I found it, straightened it out and put it on, ignoring him. Bill was waiting at the front door. I saw him step aside and another shadow came in, a very small one. He was Spig, the junior pickpocket.

Arvin was standing close to me again with the glass in his hand.

"I said 'No, thank you,'" I said.

The laughter went off his face and his lips stretched in a thin line.

"I said 'Have a drink'!"

He pulled back the arm and threw the drink in my face. It burned my eyes and ran down over my chin and under my shirt collar. Everybody was laughing now except Bill and me—even little Spig. I got a handkerchief out and wiped my face. When I could see, everything was red. But Bill Denton was still there. He was certainly there. And little Spig got his giggles under control long enough to point at him and yell:

"That's Bill Denton, the pitcher! He's the one hit Joey!"

All the laughing stopped. Arvin turned slowly from me, walked up to Bill and stared into his face.

"That right, punk?" he said. "You the pitcher that beaned Joey?"

Bill looked at me and wet his lips with his tongue.

"Yeah—I am," he said. "I'm sorry about—" Louis looked around at his two playmates.

"He's sorry," he said. "The boy says he's sorry."

22

The two playmates grumbled something. Louis stuck his finger against Bill's chest and poked at him.

"You'll be sorry, Junior," he said between his teeth, "if anything happens to Joey. I am Louis Arvin—Joey's brother. Maybe you ain't heard of me in your circle. You'll hear plenty if Joey don't come out of it."

This is it, Mac, now it's all right, I told myself. You've got a right to defend a kid.

I stepped in close and knocked Arvin's hand down.

"Keep your hands off the boy," I said.

He stared at me with wide eyes.

"What?" he said. "You tellin' me—Louis Arvin—?"

"I'm telling you Louis Arvin to keep your hands off the kid starting now."

Beyond him at the fountain, I could see the two junior mugs stiffening away from the counter. One of them reached inside his coat. Beyond them, in the curtained doorway of the back room I saw the big-bellied one with the cigar, leaning against the jamb, watching with a frozen face. I groaned inside. If it was going to be like that, I'd have to weasel out again. Too much risk for Bill Denton.

Kid, beat it, I thought.

He stayed.

Louis Arvin had backed away a couple of steps and his two pals moved up behind him slowly. At the far end of the counter, the old man was cleaning his fingernails with a penknife.

Arvin's eyes were restless. He had gone into a slight crouch and his wide shoulders bulged under his tight-fitting coat.

"Teacher's getting tough," he said. "He's the athletic type. We got to be careful."

One of his playmates laughed.

I felt Bill's hand on my shoulder.

"Come on, Coach," he said. "We better go."

"Right, kid," Arvin said. "You're pretty bright. Almost as bright as teacher. You better go."

Bill headed for the door and I backed toward it, watching Arvin. I had felt more helpless, but never so stupidly.

"When you come back," Arvin said as we stepped outside, "ride in an armored car. You'll need it."

I turned then and started away with Bill. Behind us rose a loud gale of laughter.

We'd gone a dozen steps when I felt a hand on my arm and the big, affable voice of the fat man with the cigar banged against my ear.

"One moment, my friend!"

I stood still, counting mentally, waiting for him to take his fat hand off my arm. I got to nine and a half before he did it, but he did it. So I looked at him. He was grinning happily around his cigar which he had not relighted. He had the false geniality of the fat man which has so long been taken for granted. There aren't any happy fat men.

"What did you want?" I asked him.

"If I had known—" he said, real big, "if I had known who you were, Coach, I would have stepped in and broken up that little—fracas. Allow me to apologize for the citizens of this ward."

"This is your ward?" I said.

He beamed on me.

"My name is Beasly—Herman Beasly. You're new in town, naturally, but around here, I'm known to one and all. They help me and I help them. Around City Hall, you know?"

"I guess I know."

I felt very tired.

"That Louis Arvin—he's a hothead. Had a little trouble—he's been away a couple of years. I hope he didn't give you the wrong impression of our citizens."

"Let's forget it," I said.

He clapped me on the shoulder. I clenched my teeth to keep them from rattling.

"That's the spirit, Coach! Now look—we all feel bad about Joey Arvin. Joey's one of our boys. Nice of you to come around to see him. But when you want to come again—just give me a ring, eh? I'll see to it nobody gives you any trouble. Here's my card."

He held out a smudged business card and I put it in my pocket without looking at it.

"O.K.," I said. "I'll remember."

He slugged me again in the shoulder.

"No hard feelings, Coach?" he roared.

"No—hard—feelings," I said.

He waddled away toward the cigar store, chuckling. Bill had been standing off a way, waiting, and I rejoined him now. We walked two blocks in silence. Bill spoke first.

"I think you could have beaten him, Coach, in a fair fight," he said.

I grunted something. My hands were still clenching and relaxing at my sides and I kept trying to quiet them down.

"Anyway," he said, "thanks for trying to help me."

"*Por nada*," I said.

"What?"

"Nothing. It's something I heard once."

"What does it mean?"

"I forget."

After a while he said:

"That brother of Joey's—he thinks I hit Joey on purpose, doesn't he? That's why you told me not to go up."

"He's just a wise punk looking for trouble."

"He almost got it too," Bill said. "I bet you could have smeared him, Coach."

My father can lick your father with one hand, I thought. Only thing, Pop ain't allowed to fight any more. Weak heart. Weak—

I thought of a string of dirty words and spoke each one slowly and distinctly in my mind. Then I swallowed some more of the red wire and because I hadn't been paying attention to what Bill had been saying, I said, "Huh?"

"I said, 'I guess this is where we split up.'"

We were standing on a busy corner, where a streetcar went north and south and a bus went east and west. It was a direct route out of the downtown business district, and traffic was heavy.

"Oh," I said.

"I usually take the Number Eighteen bus. I guess you go the other way."

"That is correct," I said. "I go the other way."

"You all right, Coach?"

"Sure I'm all right."

"I'm sorry about him throwing that Coke at you."

"I'll send him the cleaning bill," I said.

He laughed, but not very hard and not for long.

"I should have gone up there," he said. "I should have seen Joey."

"You'll straighten it out with Joey all right."

He shook his head slowly.

"There's another reason—besides the thing about me hitting him in the head."

"Oh?"

His face was taut and frowning.

"Coach," he said, "Joey's heading for trouble. He could turn out like his big brother Louis if he doesn't—wise up. I found out some things—"

He sounded somewhat prissy and I guess I was impatient.

"What kind of things?"

"Well—things. Listen, Coach, if you see him before I get a chance, would you tell him—I found out some things about the Blue Grotto and the whole organization—" He broke off, then finished it quickly.

"Will you tell Joey, Coach?"

"Sure. Maybe you could tell me something."

"What?"

"Have you ever heard Joey—or anybody—mention a 'Mr. Smith'?"

His face was serious, thoughtful and respectful, like the kid he was inside. But I could have sworn a curtain had dropped between me and his eyes.

"Mr.—Smith?" he said.

"That's right."

"I don't know... I know some people named Smith." I let it drop. He had some reason. It wasn't time yet.

"All right," I said, "see you at school."

I started away, then turned back.

"Will you do me a favor?" I said to him. "Will you not go down to that neighborhood again?"

He looked at me.

"You're the best pitcher I've got," I said. "I can't spare you."

He blushed some.

"O.K.," he said, "if you say so. But I'm not afraid."

My stomach tried to turn over, but missed.

"So long, Mr. Donnelly," he said.

Mr. Donnelly yet.

I crossed the street and waited a while for a streetcar. By the time I got to my own corner, in a semi-commercial section, it was nearly dark. There was a bakery with a small lunch counter and I went in and ordered a peanut butter sandwich and a glass of milk. Halfway through the sandwich, I thought of Louis Arvin and my stomach jumped again. I finished the milk and left. I picked up a paper at the newsstand and walked the half block to my apartment building, an old, comfortable place in an old, comfortable neighborhood.

It was dark in the vestibule and I didn't see the two of them sitting on the steps. If they hadn't moved, I'd have walked right over them. I stepped back quickly, hoping Louis Arvin had followed me home. But my luck hadn't even begun to change. They were two of my bosses and they looked far out of character, sitting there on the steps, one of them dangling a pair of rimless glasses, the other, a conservative felt hat between his knees.

The one with the hat was Austin Clark, Principal of the West Avenue High School. He was the guy who had talked the city fathers and the Board of Education into hiring me. The other was Dr. Morton Stein, a psychiatrist, consultant to the Board of Education. They were both men of some dignity, though not stuffy, and it looked funny to see them on my steps that way. That is, it looked funny for a moment. Then it began to look very unfunny and tiresome.

"Good evening, gentlemen," I said. "I guess it's time for you to get another boy."

There was a pause and then Clark, the principal, said, "I beg your pardon?"

Always a good line to stall with, I thought.

"Since you're here," I said then, "come on up and have a drink."

They followed me up the stairs to my apartment on the second floor.

CHAPTER FOUR

My first drink went down in a hurry and I mixed a second while Clark and Dr. Stein were still savoring theirs. They sat side by side on the davenport, watching me. With his glasses catching the light, Stein looked a little like a cockeyed owl. Clark was a young fellow, husky and friendly in the face, but worried now.

I myself was pacing the floor. I had to have some kind of exercise. Halfway through the second drink, I managed to get started.

"It just isn't my kind of work," I said. "Besides, if you'll excuse me, I don't know how you expect one lousy shamus to solve the entire problem of juvenile delinquency in a strange city of two hundred thousand people."

Nobody answered and I went on with it.

"I'm a guy," I said, "goes around collecting bills and guarding other people's jewelry. So I got mixed up in a couple of murder cases and got some publicity. I don't go around looking for them. I don't know anything about kids—teen-age vice—all that. And even if I did—what can I do? A dull jerk of a schoolteacher. Begging your pardon, Dr. Clark, but I'm even a fake schoolteacher."

I finished the drink, started to make a third, then put the glass down. I'm not a drinking man, but those two had helped. I swung around and looked at them, as nearly face to face as you can look at two men at the same time.

"So I think maybe my end of the noble experiment is a flop and I am willing to resign, as of now."

They sat there, staring into space. Dr. Stein took off his glasses and twirled them in the air. He looked into his glass, then finally at me and said in his German accent:

"You are the most not-afraid man I met ever. What has happened, that now you feel like such a failure?"

I looked at them separately this time. I had hoped they wouldn't go into it, that they would just accept my decision. I didn't feel like talking about it. But then I figured we were in it together and maybe they had some explanation coming.

"I went to see Joey Arvin," I said.

Clark jumped right in.

"How is he?"

"He'll be all right, I think."

I told them about the visit, about Francie, about Louis. Then I told them about meeting Bill Denton in the cigar store and everything that happened in there. After I got through telling it I got myself another drink. The telling had changed it. I began to think it was a little silly to put on such a show over it. I couldn't look Dr. Stein in the eye for a while. When I tried, he had put his glasses on again and I couldn't tell whether I was looking him in the eye or not.

"You showed wonderful restraint," Clark said.

"Maybe too much," said Stein.

"Too much for my stomach," I said.

"Exactly." The doctor leaned forward and set his empty glass on the floor between his feet. "Tell me something. What feelings do you think young Denton had when he left you on that corner?"

"I think he had the feeling that if he should ever have to hire a body-guard, he would do plenty of shopping around."

"But maybe not," he said. "There is evidence that Bill Denton has identified strongly with you."

"This is good?"

"This is inevitable. It happens all the time, especially to athletic coaches and English teachers. You can expect also the girls to fall in love with you."

"Donovan forbid," I said.

"I beg your pardon?"

"Nothing. I was referring to an old friend."

"I get it," Clark said. "Lieutenant Donovan of the Chicago police."

"Oh yes," Dr. Stein said. "The great cop."

"He is a great cop!" I said, flaring up.

Dr. Stein smiled.

"I don't deny it. Donovan is a kind of hero to you, is it not so?"

"If a man can have a hero today—that's right."

"So. You would like to be a great cop—like Donovan. This is identifi-cation. This is Bill Denton and you."

"Where do the girls come in?" I said.

He laughed silently.

"They'll come. I don't mean like moths around a flame. But from a distance they will admire you secretly with a consuming passion. They will even dream about you—and after feel guilty."

He stopped laughing.

29

"I tell you this because once in a while, a girl might break over. She might not keep it such a secret. When that happens, maybe you'll be prepared."

"I still don't know why."

"Someday I will try to explain why. But Dr. Clark hasn't time for lectures. Eh, Dr. Clark?"

Clark shifted in his seat.

"We stopped by, Mac," he said, "because you'd said you were going to visit Joey Arvin and I wanted to know how he is. Then, your remark about wanting to—resign—that threw me off—"

"You don't have to be polite," I said. "If you meant 'quit,' then that's what we better call it."

"You still feel you want to—quit?"

"I feel I'm not getting anywhere. And if I get pushed around any more, I'm afraid I won't show such wonderful restraint."

"What did you expect to accomplish—in this time?"

"I—don't know."

And that was the truth if ever I'd heard it.

Clark got up and started walking around. Watching him, I had no trouble picturing him as an All-American end ten years before—Northwestern, Purdue, somewhere—and I could guess how big a sale he'd made to the city fathers when he got them to hire me, a private detective, as a substitute teacher and undercover man. It must have been his personality. Maybe it was his personality that had sold me on taking the job.

Well, his personality would certainly have to go to work now.

"It's no time for speeches," he said. "I can guess how hard it's been for you. But I'd hate to see the—experiment—fold up so soon. It's not really such a 'noble' experiment, just a new kind of approach. Maybe it was all a dream. Maybe if you dream too big you can't handle it—like swallowing too much water."

"I don't know about water," I said, "but there are some things a certain type of guy can't swallow much of."

Dr. Stein rumbled something in his throat, started to talk, then closed his mouth and stared at me through his glasses.

"Will you think it over, Mac?" Clark said, facing me. "Will you think it over tonight? Just tonight." He glanced at Stein again. "Of course, if you're really set on it, I can clear it all right. I don't want you to worry about my end of it. But if you would think it over—" It felt like a trap, but what could I say?

Dr. Stein rose and picked up his glass, set it carefully on the table. Clark got his hat.

"All right," I said. "I'll think it over."

"Thanks," Clark said. "Doctor—?"

"Yah—" Stein said vaguely. Then, "Maybe, Mac, you were over—what is it—conscientious today. Maybe you wouldn't have to hold back so hard. If you want to hit a man like Louis Arvin, maybe you should hit him."

"Maybe I could go look him up and hit him right now," I said.

"Right now it wouldn't help you. There's a time to hit and a time not to hit. You know about this. I wish I had known sooner in my life—like you."

"Good night," Clark said. "Thanks for thinking it over."

"I'll think it over," I said. "Good night, gentlemen." I closed the door, turned off the light, took off my coat and shoes and lay down on the davenport to think it over—the noble experiment.

Hell, I thought, kids always got in trouble. I got in trouble myself. My old man got in trouble when he was a kid and his old man before him. In those days, of course, things moved slower. You could swipe a team of horses and tear through the streets, turn over the buggy and maybe break an arm or leg, but what else? Nobody else got hurt. Today, you could get in a hotrod, go a hundred and five miles an hour down the middle of the street and kill eighteen people besides yourself.

But that wasn't the kind of trouble Austin Clark was working on. They had really had it in this town the last few years—narcotics, gang wars, rape, even killings. The kid gangs were organized and efficient. Clark knew enough to realize they had professional help. The D.A. and the cops knew it too, but Clark wanted to concentrate on that tie-up between the grown-up professionals and the kids—a sort of "There's no such thing as *juvenile* delinquency" approach. He knew other stuff entered into it, naturally—ignorance in parents, wars, slums—all that and more. But that was long-term stuff and in the meantime, you had to try to keep the kids alive. And it made pretty good sense that if you could once trace and pinpoint the link between the professionals—find out who was bossing the show—and the kids, and beat the drum loud enough, you could maybe get some action in the criminal end of it.

So that was the end of it that Clark had figured was a job for a guy like me. If he could find a man who could double as an athletic coach, to get the kids on his side, and who also had spent some time in the dingier corners of the world, he might find one of those links. He knew that would only be the beginning. Once we found the link, he'd have to fight like a tiger to get anything done about it. Because it was one thing to find it and a different thing to make it stick. But with luck, it might work.

Anyway, he'd sold it—to those politicians and then to me. I hadn't been in on the original sale, but I was present all right when it almost flopped, when it looked for a few minutes as if all the build-up, the groundwork, the negotiation and the argument had gone for absolutely nothing...

They had a nice modern City Hall in this town and the D.A.'s office was roomy, with plenty of light and plenty of deep leather chairs to sit in. The D.A. was a big gray-haired guy of fifty with a harassed expression. He and Dr. Stein were waiting when Clark, who had met me at the station, and I went in. Also waiting was this other man—a David Cameron, attorney and prominent civic leader. He was big shot with all the trimmings, right down to the shock of white hair and the *pince-nez.* A small, almost delicate guy, but with a wiry toughness underneath. I looked at him and I thought, This guy is against me.

Sure, it was hunch, but it was a strong hunch and as soon as the introductions were over and the D.A. started to talk, it was confirmed.

"I called in Mr. Cameron," he said, "because I didn't see how we could possibly deal with the total situation without benefit of his experience and advice."

Austin Clark smiled and shook hands with Cameron, but I saw him come alert. He'd worked his fanny off to get us to this point. The contracts were ready to be signed and he'd figured everything was wrapped up. Now the D.A. had thrown him a curve.

"I'm sure Mr. Cameron understands the problem as well as anyone," Clark said.

Cameron acknowledged the salute.

"I'm in the embarrassing position," he said, "of a man who perhaps protests too late. But I knew nothing about this plan till MacDonald (the D.A.) called me this morning."

He swung in his chair and smiled at me. He had plenty of charm, but it was clear that he could be deadly in a fight.

"I've nothing against you, sir," he said to me. "I respect your talents. I think that if our problem with juvenile delinquency could be solved in this way, you would be the man to do it."

Clark picked him up quickly.

"You're saying, Mr. Cameron, that we can't solve it this way?"

"That's what I'm saying," Cameron said. "You're treating it like a job of espionage. But it's not spies we're after. It's boys—and girls. How far do you think you'll get once these youngsters find out you've set a private detective on them?"

"There's more to it—" Clark started, but the D.A. waved him silent.

"Let Mr. Cameron finish," he said.

Cameron got up and paced the floor. He had a dignity all the more impressive because of his small size. He looked too delicate to tackle any kind of problem, let alone the one we were speaking of.

"I've worked with these boys for years," he said. "I've founded boys' clubs—talked with the boys, watched them, counseled them. I know something about how they think, what they feel. I predict you won't get away with your undercover approach for three weeks. You can't fool them the way you can fool adults. They can smell a phony ten blocks away—"

"Mr. Cameron—" Clark said sharply.

Cameron smiled again, gestured toward me.

"I do not say this gentleman is a phony. It's only your method I'm criticizing. Among other things, I doubt that it's legal."

He was staring brightly at the D.A. The D.A. squirmed some.

"There are some questions—" he mumbled, "but at least, they're all open—"

"I won't start an argument about that," Cameron said. "In fact—" he smiled once more, flashing white, straight teeth, "I'm not here to argue at all. But Jim MacDonald called me in and I tried to give you my honest opinion. If you go ahead with it, naturally, you'll have my cooperation."

He set an expensive fedora carefully on his white head, shook hands all round, murmured something like goodbye and left the office, waving at us with a limp, almost effeminate gesture.

There was a long silence and then Dr. Stein cleared his throat. That woke me up and I excused myself so they could talk it over. I pounded the tile floor of a gleaming white corridor for fifteen minutes, hoping they would at least buy me a return-trip ticket to Chicago. And finally the D.A. stuck his head out and called me in.

He had the contracts all laid out on his desk and I was invited to sign them. I picked up the pen he offered me and looked across the desk at him. He didn't look nervous any more. He looked a little grim.

"What about the other gentleman?" I said.

"He's a distinguished citizen," the D.A. said, "a man of ability and integrity. But he is not the District Attorney, nor the Mayor nor the Board of Education. I am inclined personally to go along with him. But I've been overruled. If you'll sign, please—" That had been six weeks before, and as far as any of us could tell, in spite of what Cameron had said about the kids spotting a phony set-up, we were still in the clear and unknown.

Six weeks, I thought, lying there on the davenport, and what's been accomplished? Tell us about that, shamus.

You spent two weeks of the time trying to get Joey Arvin out for baseball. Joey was the leader of his own gang, the boy we had to cultivate. If we could make an athletic hero out of him, instead of a potential hoodlum hero, we'd begin to get a grip on the situation.

So what happened? You got him on the team. You built him up, you got him hit in the head with a ball and laid up and now what? What now, shamus? Where's the focus now, the handle? What are you working on? Nothing. There is not any handle to take hold of.

Only there was too. There was the little girl, the one with the yellow hair that they found in a trash can in Joey's neighborhood. You saw the pictures, didn't you, shamus? Didn't you see them? The trash can was the place for her all right after whoever it was—or were—got through with her. They rounded up all the sex offenders they knew of in the city, but every one was clear. So they decided it was a kids' job and they told the papers and kept telling it till people believed it. Then there was a big stink about juvenile delinquency and they rounded up kids by the truckload. But they never found out who killed the little girl.

So here we were. Running around to visit a kid with a busted head and taking lip and nonsense from a smalltime hood like Louis Arvin and a pudgy ward heeler like Beasly.

Big deal.

It wouldn't work. It couldn't work and we all knew it now. All we had to do was face it. And if they wanted the money back that they'd paid me so far, then all right too. It might take a little while, but they'd get it back.

I climbed up from the davenport, feeling like a wrestler with his legs caught in a fish net, and found my way to the table where the bottle was. And then the telephone started to ring.

It rang quite a while. I poured whisky in the glass, went to the kitchen for some water, filled it up, took a couple of sips and finally, when the ringing wouldn't stop, picked up the phone. It was a woman speaking.

"Mr.—Donnelly?"

"Yes, ma'am."

"This is Francine Arvin."

My hand tightened on the phone and I forced it to relax.

"Yes?" I said.

"I'm worried—I wondered—could you come down—"

"What if I start asking questions?"

There was a pause. Then she said, "I guess I asked for that."

Behind her voice I could hear jazz music and the rattle of dishes.

"What's got you worried?" I said.

"It's Joey. He's not home."

"Where are you, Francie?"

"At work. I went home for a few minutes to check up—"

"Well, maybe he just stepped out for a breath of air."

"There was something about a party. I'm worried about him. That Stella—maybe you don't know about those parties."

"Maybe you ought to tell me about them."

"I can't talk here any more—on the phone. Could you come down where I work?"

"You don't feel like calling a cop?"

"Do you think I feel like that?"

"All right, Francie," I said. "Where is it?"

She told me. She told me carefully and well and after she hung up I changed my clothes, to get rid of the stains from the Coke Louis Arvin had thrown at me, got some money out of the bureau drawer, checked my pockets to make sure I had nothing that would identify me as anything except a jerk schoolteacher, and left the apartment. Looking back at the building as I walked away, I didn't feel as if I were leaving much. It had never seemed like home.

CHAPTER FIVE

She worked in a dump all right. She had been absolutely honest about that. One of those frantically dingy oases catering to the playboys of the depressed areas, who are distinguished from rich playboys by the fact that they have less money to spend and expect just as much for it. Come to think of it, I guess there isn't any real difference except in the quantity of money that changes hands.

There was a jukebox at the far end of a row of booths on one side and on the other side, a bar. Between the booths and the bar was a row of tables. The booths were full and the bar was filled, but the tables were all empty when I went in. I pulled up a chair near the front door, where the air was relatively fresh, and waited.

I had to wait for some time. There was another waitress in the place, but she was busy with some guy at the bar who kept patting her here and there and she couldn't seem to tear herself away. Or maybe Francie had already given her the sign that I belonged to her. Finally she came in sight, approaching along the row of booths, the Madonna of the West Side, Miss Francine Arvin.

It was quite a gauntlet she had to run but she made it unscathed, dodging a poke here, a pinch there, tossing her head at a raucous shout. I had to admire her technique. Then I guessed that was one of the tricks of that trade and naturally you'd learn it if you wanted to stay in it.

She stood beside the table, holding a cocktail tray in one hand.

"It will look better," she said, "if there's a drink in front of you. I'll buy it."

"I can afford to buy it," I said.

"Well, you don't have to drink it."

"Any reason I shouldn't drink it?"

"No. I didn't know—"

"All right, Francie. If you'll bring me a bourbon in water, we'll get along fine. One for yourself, if you like."

She went away. When she came back she had two highballs on the tray. She set them down, then set herself down on a chair across from me.

I tasted the drink and it was pretty good. I looked at her.

"I told the bartender it was for a friend," she said.

36

I was a little embarrassed.

"What about Joey?" I said.

"That Stella—I know I yelled at her today. Will you forget what I said about—?"

"About reefers?"

"You know what a reefer is, Mr. Donnelly?"

"Yes, I know."

"Stella was with Joey when I left for work. I didn't think much about it at first, and then down here, somebody mentioned a kids' party in the neighborhood. When I got a break, I ran home to check and Joey wasn't there."

"Maybe he's all right. A little party—maybe he feels better than we think."

Her face sagged a little. I thought how soon it could develop a permanent sag if she stayed in this place, with her responsibilities.

"Joey's awful sick, Mr. Donnelly. I didn't tell you—I was afraid—like I said. But this afternoon, he got out of bed to go to the bathroom and he fell down. He said he got dizzy and couldn't see anything."

"Yeah?"

"Besides—you don't know about those parties. This isn't any uptown dancing class. This is a brawl. The whole works."

"With reefers?"

"Maybe, and more. Those kids lose their heads."

I let it sit there a while, looking it over.

"Mr. Donnelly—I'm scared."

She was leaning across the table and she had plenty of equipment in her sales kit, but the only part of it she was using was her eyes. Everything in her eyes was for real.

"What did you think I could do?" I said.

"I thought—maybe if you would go over there and talk to Joey. He likes you. He told me once. You're the only one at school he ever said that about."

"Apparently the feeling is not unanimous in the family," I said.

She didn't get it right away; then her eyes fell.

"You mean Louis."

"He pushed me around some this afternoon—not only in your apartment—and I took it."

She looked at me straight then.

"Why?"

"Why what?"

"Why did you just take it? You look like a man who can take care of himself."

"Maybe because—" I swallowed, "there are other ways than fighting, Francie."

"Not down here there aren't," she said.

I finished my drink and pushed the glass to one side.

"All right," I said, "I'll do what I can about Joey if you'll let me call a doctor to have a look at him."

She looked at the table.

"For free," I said. "He won't send a bill."

"What—" she started weakly, then rallied and came out with it. "What if Joey's a little—hopped up or something? The doctor will know. What will he do?"

"He won't do anything, except to treat Joey. I promise."

She gave in.

"All right," she said. "Call the doctor. But please do something about Joey."

"Where can I find the party?"

She told me.

"Is there a phone?" I asked.

She pointed toward the back. I started in that direction, then stopped to face her as she got up from the table.

"I'm asking the doctor to meet me here. If I can get Joey away from the party, I'll bring him down here first."

"All right," she said.

"One more thing."

She held herself in, but her eyes were telling me to get going.

"Yes?" she said.

"Who is Mr. Smith?"

I had done wrong again. It was clear by the sudden dead look in her eyes, the stiffening resistance in the way she stood, held her hands and her head.

"I don't know any 'Mr. Smith,'" she said. "Please—about Joey—"

"Yes, Francie," I said, leaving her.

I went to where a telephone hung on the wall behind the jukebox. I found Dr. Stein's number in my wallet and dialed it.

While I stood there waiting for him to come on, the front door opened and a woman came in, hesitated, looking around, then walked quietly to one of the tables and sat down. I wouldn't have paid any attention except that she was very beautiful, obviously well heeled and as out of place in this joint as a bird of paradise growing in a stable. She had silver hair and the saloon lights gleamed in it.

Stein came on the line and I gave him a quick rundown on what was up and asked if he'd meet me at the joint to take a look at Joey. There was some hesitation, but then he said, "Of course, Mac."

"And alone," I said. "Nobody with you."

"I understand."

He hung up and when I turned from the telephone Francie was behind me, watching. I put a hand on her arm.

"I'll check back with you. Try not to worry."

She didn't say anything but we were looking at each other in a new way.

As I passed the table where the silver-haired woman sat, she glanced up and our eyes met. She smiled faintly and I touched my hat. I thought about her all the way to the street. She made pleasant thinking.

I walked two blocks in the wrong direction before I got oriented and it took me fifteen minutes at a brisk pace to reach the building where Francie had told me I'd find the party.

There were steps leading down to a basement apartment. It was a warm night, the door was open and there wasn't any doubt about the fact that a party was going on. They had a phonograph in there and you could hear the beat of the music, shuffling feet and a murmur of voices. Now and then the voices would rise in a shout or a laugh.

I stood there a while and a boy and girl came out of the door, holding each other tightly and disappeared in the shadows under the stairs. I went down the steps slowly.

From the doorway, I looked through a curtain of smoke at a crowd of milling kids, wrapped in each other's arms, swaying to the beat of some lowdown music. I couldn't see the phonograph. There were other kids draped on some ragged sofas around the walls. The place looked as if it had once been lived in, but certainly now it would not be used for anything except parties like this one. Colored paper had been pinned up here and there some time since, and there were strings of Christmas tree lights over a couple of doorways in the rear wall. The only other lights were some dim, colored bulbs in half a dozen leaning floor lamps. While I watched, a couple bumped into one of the lamps, knocking it over and putting the light out. There was some mild laughter in that corner, but otherwise it went unnoticed.

It was no place for me really. I was the original uninvited guest. But I couldn't find Joey Arvin or his girl Stella from where I stood. I waited for a break in the dancing crowd near the door and slid inside to lean against the wall, trying to focus through the smoke and the dim lights. A couple danced into me, the boy lost his balance and both of them staggered around, laughing hilariously. They were carrying quite a load. If they noticed me, they didn't show any signs of it. I edged on slowly along the wall, a few feet at a time, wishing somebody would turn on some more lights. But nobody did. It was impossible to pick out faces more than a dozen feet away and the way they kept dancing and milling around, there wasn't any one face in position long enough to be recognized. After a few minutes they all looked like the same kid—that is, the boys all looked like the same boy and likewise with the girls. I reached a corner of the room and almost tripped over the end of a sofa, on which two couples were engaged in some very heavy necking.

The air in the place was bad, what with the smoke and the bodies and the fact that the door was the only source of air. There were some small windows high up along one wall, but they were closed. I doubted that they had ever been open. There were iron bars on the outside and beyond them, through the foggy night light, I could see the wall of the building across the alley.

The ones on the sofa didn't pay any attention to me and I stood there for a long time, waiting, studying the kids who floated by in the dance, waiting to find Joey and Stella. The dancing never stopped. When the music ended, they went right on shuffling and the next record, even when it had a different beat, didn't seem to change the rhythm. I had begun to sweat heavily and I took off my hat and wiped the band of it with one hand and put it back on.

It must have been my movement that attracted some attention. All of a sudden there were three kids standing in front of me, regarding me with great hostility and suspicion. I didn't recognize any of them. They were a little older than Joey or Bill, around nineteen, maybe twenty.

I took my time, got my hat straight on my head and settled my shoulders against the wall. None of the trio said a word. I kept my eyes moving, watching the dancing couples. After a long time, one of them cracked. He shouldered himself away from the other two, who closed in behind him, and approached me slowly. He had begun already to adopt some of the mannerisms of his older models, such as Louis Arvin.

"Got business here, Dad?" he said.

"I'm looking for somebody," I said.

"Maybe you'd like us to turn on some more lights."

"That would help," I said.

He looked around, probably to make sure the other two were still there. And they were. They had been well schooled.

"Who are you looking for, Dad?" he said then, swinging back to me.

"Joey Arvin."

"Joey—?"

He looked around again. One of his companions shook his head slightly. The spokesman turned to me once more.

"Ain't here," he said. "Maybe he's home."

"He's not home," I said. "I tried that."

He shrugged.

"Then I don't know, Dad."

He made no move to go. They had maybe figured me for a city cop, nosing around, then hadn't been sure. Still it was clear enough I had got as far into the party as I was to get, if they could control it.

The talkative one looked at his two pals and they all shrugged. He tried conversation again.

"Look, Dad—if it's all the same to you, we got a party here. If you got an invitation—"

"No," I said. "I just wanted to speak to Joey Arvin for a few minutes."

"Why?"

"He's one of my ballplayers."

The hostility in his face deepened.

"You a schoolteacher?"

"That's right."

The other two moved in closer. Since I wasn't a cop, they didn't have to figure so many angles. One of them found his voice.

"Working overtime?" he said nastily.

"Joey got hurt," I said. "I wouldn't want to see him get any worse."

"Neither would we, Dad," said the first one. "I tell you the truth, neither would we."

The two young lieutenants moved casually but efficiently past the leader until they had me flanked, one on each side against the wall. The third was directly in front of me now. He looked into my face for a moment, then jerked his hand toward the door.

"Out," he said.

The two flankers began jostling my arms, pressing in. I could mix it up with them right there and make a big thing of it, or I could retreat once more, play it smart, look for another way in and keep everybody relaxed. I was in favor of relaxation, but I was getting awfully sick of the retreat routine.

"Well," I said, swallowing it once more, "if Joey isn't here—"

"Like we said, Dad, he ain't here."

I started toward the door and a dancing couple staggered in front of me. The chief bouncer pushed them savagely out of the way and they stared at him in surprise, glanced at me curiously and went back to each other's arms. One of the two aides gave me a push from behind and we went on to the door. I walked through it and the three of them bunched up in it, watching me.

"So long, Dad," said one of them. "Come back next week. Don't call us. We'll call you."

"Good night," I said and went up the steps with what I hoped was the full-blown dignity of a respectable schoolteacher.

The street was dark and empty and I walked to the alley that ran along the side of the building and turned into it. I could see the colored lights through the dirty panes of the barred windows just above the street level. I could hear the music, though it faded as I went farther on. I remembered the two doors in the rear wall of the room and tried to estimate the distance to the partition. I went as far as I could reasonably guess the main room extended and looked on along the wall. There were more windows. I squatted down to look through them, but shades had been drawn over them and I couldn't see anything. There was a faint glow behind one of the shades so I knew there were lights inside. I went on along the wall, looking for a door.

I found it ten feet beyond the last window, a heavy wooden door with a metal frame and a frosted glass panel. Some pieces had been broken out of the panel, but it was dark beyond them and I couldn't make anything out. I could no longer hear the thud of the music from the front room.

I tried the door and it was unlocked. I went through it into a damp, sour-smelling vestibule and there were a couple of trash cans, filled to overflowing. I kicked the stuff out of the way and walked along a narrow hall to another door on my left. It, too, was unlocked. I went in and lit a match.

This had been the kitchen of the apartment I had been thrown out of. There was an old stove, a sink with a wooden shelf beside it and some cupboards hung on one wall. The stove was evidently still connected. I could smell leaking gas. Beside the sink shelf was a swinging door that probably opened on a bedroom that would be between the kitchen and the dance floor. There were sounds in it, faint and sporadic, but I couldn't tell what made them.

I did know I was not alone in the kitchen. I don't know how I could know, but you know. You learn.

The match burned my finger and I dropped it. I found another and scratched it into flame. I took a deep breath and looked down.

I held the breath for as long as it took the match to burn me again, dropped it, exhaled slowly and lit a third. I went down on one knee, stiffly, to confirm the identity of the boy who lay sprawled on the floor at my feet. It didn't take long. It was Bill Denton and he was dead.

He was lucky to be dead. He had been very badly used.

CHAPTER SIX

Somebody had turned up the volume on the phonograph and I could feel the heavy beat vibrating through the dark. I burned up a couple of matches and got it through my head that I couldn't do anything for Bill Denton. It wasn't easy. It was hard to remember that I'd seen him only a few hours earlier, alive, walking on straight legs, not afraid, fully alive, ready to pitch the next day's ball game. Now all the aliveness had spilled out of him, along with the ragged blotches of blood from half a dozen wounds in his face and neck and another on his shirt front, not too big. He'd been that lucky. When they'd finally got around to finishing him off, it couldn't have taken too long. But a boy dies hard and he must have known it was coming.

I fought down the rage and sickness and looked through his pockets. There wasn't much—a slim wallet with a dollar in it and an ID card; some odds and ends that meant nothing, and a many-creased scrap of paper with something scribbled on it in pencil. I lit a match to read it.

It was the beginning of a letter, written on a piece of ruled paper torn from a notebook. There were only a couple of lines. The letter had never got finished.

Mr. David Cameron:
(There was an address on Riverside Drive.)

Dear Uncle David:
   I don't know how to start—if only it weren't for *her*—

And that was all of it.

I started to replace it in his pocket, then stuck it in my own coat pocket.

One of his hands was loosely clenched and I set my teeth and opened his fingers. Something rolled off his hand onto the floor and I found it and looked at it in the match light. A small pearl button such as you might find on a woman's blouse. There were some white threads hanging from the wire loop that attached it. I put it back in his hands and closed his fingers over it. The cops would need it. They would like to have the letter too, but they could wait for that.

From the room beyond the swinging door, I heard a suppressed giggle, feminine and feline. The rage climbed again, knotting in my throat, and I

43

stepped over the broken figure on the floor and pushed through the swinging door.

It was a bedroom, as I had guessed. A sagging double bed took up most of the space. There was a battered dresser, with mirror, beyond the foot of the bed. A dim light burned in a lamp on the dresser. It was light enough to show me Stella Perino, lying on her back on the bed, gazing at a scrap of paper she held with both hands close to her face. Beside her, apparently asleep, lay Joey Arvin with the dirty bandage still on his head.

Stella looked at me blankly for a moment. Then her head swung quickly and whatever she had been holding fluttered out of sight. She straightened up, swung her legs over the edge of the bed and pulled her skirt down over her knees. Her red mouth was distorted.

"Mr.—Donnelly!" she squeaked.

"Get up," I said, feeling my teeth grind as I spoke. "Get up from the bed."

Her mouth moved but she said nothing. She didn't get up.

I was moving toward her with my hand out when I managed to check myself once more. "There's a time to hit and a time not to hit," Dr. Stein had said. "You know about this."

I hoped I did.

"Come on," I said to her. "We've got a trip to take."

"But—" she started it out loud, then dropped to a whisper when I gestured. "Why—?" she said then, giggling. "We just got here."

"Joey's got to get to bed," I said.

"Joey's all right. He's just asleep."

"Well, wake him up and let's go."

She pouted. I almost slapped her then, but her eyes slid past me, widened suddenly and she put one hand to her mouth. Then she struggled to make a recovery. I turned and looked at the dresser. Near the lamp were a glass of water, a cigarette lighter and a cheap aluminum spoon. Something like a bear-trap snapped together inside me.

"Is he high?" I said.

"No! He's just asleep."

"Don't play games, Stella. I'm going to get him out of here and I'd like some help."

"He's all right, I tell you."

"What's the stuff on the dresser?"

She opened her mouth, closed it again and shrugged.

"It was here. I don't know—Joey's all right. Why can't you let him sleep?"

I went around the bed and reached for Joey's left arm. He was wearing a leather jacket and I started to push the sleeve up. Stella leaned across him, grabbed the sleeve and looked at me frantically.

"Leave him alone. He's all right!"

"Is he high?" I said.

She started to cry.

"Do I look high?" she said.

"I'm not asking about you. I'm asking about Joey."

She cried some more. I shook her shoulder.

"Stop it. I have to know, Stella."

"His head hurt," she said. "I just gave him a little bit—it was cut—not enough to hurt anything—"

"What was it?"

"Nothing. It was just—"

"What was it?"

Her whisper was from far away.

"White stuff," she said.

"How long ago did you hit him?"

"I don't know. Please—"

"Half an hour? An hour?"

"I don't remember. Leave me alone!"

She started to crawl away from me across the bed and I grabbed her. She fought me, scratching at my face with her nails, breathing in hard, frightened gasps. I got hold of her arms and held her till she quieted down.

"Listen, Stella," I said. "I have to know, because we have to get him up and out of here and I don't want any disturbance. If he has to be carried, then all right."

"I don't know. Maybe half an hour."

"You hit yourself too?"

"No. I'm not on it."

"All right. Wake him up."

She just sat there, leaning back from me, staring, her red lips parted. I could smell it now on her breath. She was loaded too, but with alcohol.

I eased her back out of the way, got an arm under Joey's shoulders and lifted him. He groaned. I massaged the back of his neck gently. Pretty soon he came around some and tried to push me away, but his push was weak. Stella sat helplessly on the bed, staring at me. Joey's mouth opened and I clapped my hand over it to keep him from yelling. If he'd worked his way into a bad dream, he could wake up screaming but good.

"Anybody likely to come in here?" I asked Stella.

She giggled.

"I locked the door."

"Have you seen Bill Denton tonight?"

Her red mouth pursed.

"Who?"

"You heard me."

"Bill—Denton? The pitcher—?" It appeared to break on her like a great light.

"He's an uptown kid! He wouldn't be down here."

"Nobody brought him down?"

"Not that I know of."

"All right. Let's go."

I took my hand away from Joey's mouth. He rolled his eyes up at me, then his head fell back against my arm. His mouth and jaw were stupidly slack.

"Go 'way," he muttered. "Lea'me alone."

"Wake up, Joey," I said. "We've got to go."

He tried again to push me away. I jerked my head at Stella.

"Come around here and help me," I said. "I'm not fooling. You'll be a sick girl if you don't come along."

"What's wrong, Mr. Donnelly?" she said, getting off the bed, worried now. "They going to raid the party or something?"

"Maybe," I said. "Maybe that's it."

She moved around the bed slowly, holding onto the foot rail, staggering a little, her beautiful little face muddled now and out of shape. She managed to get one of Joey's arms around her shoulders and I lifted him off the bed onto his feet. The three of us started back around the bed in a crazy, wallowing, staggering ballet, banging against everything in sight. Joey wouldn't come around and I had to keep hitching him up to prevent the two of them from falling on the floor. We managed to get past the foot of the bed and I was reaching for the swinging door into the kitchen when I heard sound beyond it. The rear door had opened and there were quick footsteps. Then a pencil of light showed under the swinging door.

I pushed Stella against the wall, propped Joey against her with his arms hanging over her shoulders, wrapped Stella's arms around his waist and told her to hold on. Strangely, she did it. I left them there and pushed through the door into the kitchen. I wasn't careful about it. I was badly frustrated already and it didn't help a bit to see Louis Arvin crouched beside Bill Denton's body, playing a flashlight over it, or the sneer on his face when he looked up and saw me come into the room. He held the sneer for some time and then he said:

"Look who's here! This part of your class won't be showing up any more, teacher."

I'd taken my last smart crack from a cheap bum like him.

"He's already dead, Arvin," I said. "You can't kill him again."

His face could be quite ugly. It was ugly now.

"What the hell you saying, jerk?"

"No sixteen-year-old kid would do that to himself."

He rose slowly from the crouch, his eyes spitting at me.

"I ought to put you right beside him, teacher," he said.

"Better send for help."

His mouth opened and closed. If he had made any sound, it would have been a sputter. But he didn't make any sound. His right hand moved suddenly across his chest and he came at me, stepping over Denton, and there was a knife in his hand, the blade out. Like the dumb schmuck he was, he dropped the flashlight on the floor and it stayed on.

You don't throw yourself at a man with a knife. You wait him out, box with him. You keep your eye on the knife. Nothing else matters. Even a feint with his fist to the side of your head, even a blow. The chances are he can't hit you hard enough to knock you out, or even down. He's concentrating on the knife too. And he keeps his distance, knowing that if he should lose his footing, trip or lunge wrongly, he can fall on his own knife and the thing will be over in a hurry. He has the length of his arm, plus three or four inches of knife-blade and those few inches can mean the difference between life and death, when the opponent is bare-handed. If the opponent is armed, too, there are other factors.

Louis Arvin knew all this. He must have had a long training in the art of jungle fencing. He even knew that the longer he could keep me waiting, draw out the suspense, the better chance he had to rattle me, take me off base. But I had been through it before and there wasn't any way he could know that. Besides that, the only other break in my favor was the fact that he had dropped his flash and there was plenty of light glinting on the knife-blade. My eyes began to water as I watched it move in a wide, slow arc, waist high, while Arvin circled, waiting me out, his left hand dancing nervously in the air, preparing to feint, sliding on and off the rim of my vision.

The feint came quickly, as it should have, but luckily short and I was already moving my shoulders back, pivoting at the same time, when he lunged. As the blade flashed past the place where my neck had been, I used both hands on his arm, one below the bicep and one on his forearm, hard and sharp, twisting him out of line, driving him across the room in a frantic scramble. But I had not heard the arm snap nor the knife drop and I followed through behind him, pushing him on into the wall beside the stove, getting an arm around his neck from behind.

He twisted like a wet cat, waving the knife wildly at first, then trying to cut at my wrists, foolishly taking a chance with his own eyes. I tightened the pressure on his neck and the flailing stopped. There was a gurgle out of him and when I told him to drop the knife, he did it promptly. I let up on his neck, pulled him back across the floor toward the swinging door to the bedroom, and let go. He dropped like a bundle of stones, rolled over once and came up at me, growling something in his throat. I hit him twice on the chin and he fell face down on the floor. I stood there a minute, with an empty feeling, trying to get my breath back. Then I stooped, rolled him over and got my hands under his arms. I dragged him into the bedroom, got his shoulders on the bed, lifted his feet and rolled him onto it. When I straightened and turned around, Joey had released himself from Stella and was weaving his way across the room toward me. At the edge of the bed he stopped and stared down at it. After a while he looked at me, blinking rapidly to get his eyes in focus.

"That's Louis," he said hoarsely. "You did that to Louis?"

"I did that to Louis," I said. "Sometimes there's no other way. Let's go."

He stood there, shaking his muddled head. If he was coming down from his high, it probably hurt plenty.

"You can't do that to Louis—nobody—"

"All right, Joey," I said, taking his arm. "We've got to get out of here."

Stella was leaning against the wall where he had left her, her hands limp at her sides, her shoulders pressed against the peeling wallpaper, her face frightened and shapeless. Joey pushed my hand away and reeled toward her. She didn't move. His voice was plaintive.

"Stella—what's go'n on? What's—Stella—" She didn't touch him. He turned, staggering, and looked at me again.

"What's the matter? Why'nt you leave us alone?"

I went to the swinging door and pushed it open.

"I don't like this part," I said, "but I'll show you why."

He wouldn't move and I had to take his arm and push him through the door before he could see, by the light of his brother's flashlight, the mangled, sorry thing that lay on the floor. He looked for a long time and Stella moved slowly to look over his shoulder. I heard her gasp and the gasp strangled as she tried to swallow it.

"What's that?" Joey said finally.

"That's Bill Denton," I said. "Will you come along now?"

I took his arm again and urged him and he walked with me, still hanging back, his head twisting as he stared unblinking at Bill Denton's body. I looked back and Stella was following us, one hand held up in front, as if she were walking in blackness.

CHAPTER SEVEN

The walk to Francie's joint braced both of them some. Stella had got sick along the way and by the time we reached the door of the place, she was steady on her feet, but very pale. There had been absolutely no conversation during the trip. I stood them up side by side against the brick wall around the corner from the entrance.

"Stay here," I said. "Don't try to go away. If you do, there's no way I can help you any more."

They looked at me in silence.

Inside, Dr. Stein was sitting at the front table, where I had sat with Francie earlier. There was a half-full glass of beer on the table in front of him. When I told him about Bill Denton, he gave a kind of groan, took off his glasses and ran his hand heavily across his eyes. Then he put the glasses on again and looked out at me from behind them.

"What shall we do first?" he said.

I didn't like to think of it, but it had to be thought of. There wasn't anybody else to do it.

"One of us will have to call the police, anonymously," I said.

His big face was tight.

"I would do everything I can do," he said. "But if I call the police—with my accent—"

"O.K. I'll call them. Will you go out and keep an eye on Joey and Stella?"

"Of course."

We got up from the table at the same time. He went toward the front door and I headed for the phone. I found that the lovely lady with the silver hair was still with us, but she had moved from her table into a booth. She was still alone. Our eyes met again, but she lowered hers this time and there was no smile. If we were going to keep running into each other this way, I would have to have a name for her. It would have to be a high class name—like "Duchess" maybe. Duchess would do for now.

Halfway to the phone, I ran into Francie, carrying a loaded cocktail tray. When she saw me alone, her face went dead.

"Joey's outside," I said to her. "You'll have to get off and come home with us."

"I don't think—"

"You'll have to, Francie."

"All right," she said.

"We'll have to take Stella to your place and feed her some coffee. I have to talk to her."

Francie nodded.

I went past her and got to the phone. I hated it being out in the open that way, but the music was loud and that would help. I dialed Operator and asked for the police—emergency. She put me right through. A heavy voice identified itself as Precinct Eighteen and I said:

"You'll find a dead boy in the rear of an apartment on Grand Avenue near Fourteenth. There's a party in progress."

"Who is this?" he said.

I hung up. I got my wallet, found Austin Clark's number and dialed it. He didn't answer right away and my palms began to sweat. I felt somebody behind me and turned to find Francie, wearing a topcoat.

"Joey's outside," I said. "The doctor is with him."

Clark came on the line, but I held my hand over the mouthpiece and waited till Francie had gone before answering.

"I have to talk fast and brief," I said. "Bill Denton has been killed, in Joey Arvin's neighborhood. I called the police. You better get to the Mayor right away and tell him to put the hush on it. If it breaks wide open now, we'll get lost in it."

"Whatever you say, Mac. Where did you find him—so I can tell the Mayor?"

I told him and hung up. The directory hanging on a chain beside the telephone was battered and pages were leaking out of it from all angles. When I opened it, some of the pages fell out I didn't bother to pick them up. I found my way to the "C's" and ran my finger down the columns till I found Cameron, David, Attorney. The residence was on Riverside Drive. I dialed the number and waited. It rang eleven times and nobody answered. I hung up and walked past the row of booths to the door and outside. The Duchess was still there, but our eyes did not meet.

Dr. Stein, Stella, Joey and Francie were standing in a tight group. Francie had her arm around Joey, who was staring at the sidewalk.

"I have a car up the street," Dr. Stein said.

We walked up there, Stella weaving again. The car was a big sedan and I put Francie in front with Stein and got into the back with Joey and Stella. They sat upright and stiff, neither touching the other.

It was a short drive to Francie's place and there was room to park in front. I got Stella and Joey out of the car. Joey almost fell and I had to grab him quickly around the waist. Stella came along, unsteady and without direction. Francie got out without waiting for Dr. Stein and led the way. Joey straightened up some after he got inside—maybe it was the familiar smell—and started the climb under his own steam. Stella followed him. I stayed behind her, ready to catch them both if they should fall. Dr. Stein brought up the rear, a heavy black bag in his hand.

Light glowed above us as we made the last turn and started up to Francie's door. There was the sound of shuffling feet and I looked around Stella to see Louis Arvin at the head of the stairs, in shirtsleeves, glaring down at us. Francie had seen him a moment sooner and stopped dead. Joey went on climbing, bumped into Francie and stopped, leaning on the stair rail. Stella swayed and I held her arm till she got hold of the railing. Behind me, Dr. Stein rumbled in his throat.

There was some silence and then Francie spoke quietly.

"Hello, Louis."

He growled something. His voice was low, like hers, but the tension in it was more obvious. I thought about what a quick recovery he'd made. I had cooled him thoroughly back in the kitchen of that apartment. He was maybe as tough a cookie as his admirers claimed and he was very dangerous now because he had been licked by a man he thought of as a jerk and, like a wounded animal, might well attack anybody in sight without warning. Francie couldn't know he'd been licked, but she knew Louis well enough to handle him with soft hands and she went about it with considerable skill.

After the first hesitation on the stairs, she started up, moving casually and slowly, while Louis watched her. She reached the next to the last step and he snarled at her.

"Where's Joey?"

"Right here, Louis," she soothed. "Behind me."

"Get him inside," he said.

Francie went past him, turning to face him as she passed, and stood in the open doorway of the apartment. Joey followed her blindly. I gave Stella a push and she went along. I climbed the last few steps and Louis put a hand out toward my chest.

"Not you," he said.

Francie spoke from the door, still quiet, still soothing.

"Louis—he brought Joey home. He's on Joey's side."

Louis didn't answer. He was looking past me at Dr. Stein who had stopped two steps below.

"Who's that one?" he asked, pointing.

"A doctor," Francie said. "Joey's sick."

"This is as far as they go," Louis said.

Francie's tone didn't change.

"Get out of the way, Louis."

He jerked his head around and lashed out at her.

"Shut up! I say they ain't comin' in. If you let them go in there, I'll beat you up like never before."

"No you won't, Louis," she said calmly. "You'll get out of the way and let them in."

When he continued to look at her, I shifted my weight on the step and gestured to Dr. Stein to stay put.

"Get out of the way, Louis," Francie said quietly.

But Louis had had enough for the evening. He was taking no more, least of all from his sister. I saw him start, but he didn't have far to go and I had to get up off the step. He had struck Francie across the side of the head before I could reach him. When I grabbed him from behind, instead of turning, as I had expected, he plunged away from me into the apartment and I tumbled in after him, falling as I tried to avoid stepping on Francie's feet. I fell against the backs of his legs and he went down hard on his face. I managed to get up first and suck in enough air to move before he could come up at me. He started up all right, then checked himself and gave me the evil eye from a crouch. He didn't really want to fight me. With a corner of my eye, I saw Joey, his hand on the knob of the bedroom door, staring at us. Then I felt Francie's hand on my arm. She was bending down, looking in Louis's face.

"Listen, Louis," she said. "Get out of here now. Go to your room and stay there. Don't come out. If you come out and make trouble, so help me, Louis, I'll call a cop. And I know what I'm doing."

I had seldom heard words spoken more from the heart. Louis heard them too. But he went on staring at me. Francie put her hand on his chin and pulled his head around till he had to face her.

"You hear me, Louis?" she said. "Go to your room."

After a moment his eyes dropped. He pushed himself slowly to his feet, picked his coat off the back of a chair and went through a door at the side of the room. I heard the door of Joey's bedroom close softly.

Stella was standing alone near me. Dr. Stein went to Francie and looked at the side of her head without touching her.

"Did he hurt you, Miss?" he said.

"No," she said, moving away. "I'm all right."

"Joey's in there," I said, pointing to the closed door of his room.

Dr. Stein nodded and went in there. Francie stared after him for a long time, as if she had forgotten everything except how to stare at a closed door. Then she turned to me with an empty face.

"You want a drink or something?" she said.

On a small table beside the chair where Louis's coat had hung, was a half-full whisky bottle and a glass.

"No, thanks," I said. "How about some coffee?"

She shrugged out of her topcoat, threw it over the chair and crossed toward a swinging door beyond Joey's room. She was still wearing her waitress's uniform. It was not an inspired design and the original blue of it had faded almost to gray. But she wore it with an intuitive grace and I thought again of what a fine line there was between her and any girl from "uptown"—between her and the Duchess, say.

People are never born, I thought. All people are made.

And then I thought, You're some philosopher, Mac. How about a little philosophy about the job in hand? How about that?

I touched Stella's arm and we followed Francie through the swinging door.

CHAPTER EIGHT

In the kitchen, Francie had turned on a bright overhead light and set a pan of water on a gas burner. She reached into a cupboard, got down cups and a jar of instant coffee. The kitchen was small and the stove leaked badly. There was an icebox and when she opened it to get out a can of condensed milk, I saw there was little else in it. I guessed she ate her own meals on the job and maybe she fed Louis and Joey there too. There was a small table with a cracked oilcloth cover on it and three chairs and I pulled out two of the chairs, put Stella on one and sat down. Francie waited by the stove till the water began to boil. Then she made the coffee, put the cups in front of us and sat down herself across from Stella. She sat with her head resting on one hand and the steam from the coffee rose slowly, drifting across her face. Stella sat motionless beside me, staring into space.

I drank some of the coffee, burning my tongue. I waited for it to cool, drank some more. And then, because you can't stall forever, I said:

"Stella—you remember what we saw back there at the party?"

She didn't answer.

"On the floor in the kitchen, Stella. Don't you remember?"

She quivered as if somebody had run fingers lightly along her spine. Francie was watching me closely but her face showed nothing.

"Drink some of the coffee, Stella," I said. "It will help."

She lifted her head and took hold of the cup, but she couldn't seem to lift it. I lifted it for her, held it to her mouth. She took some of it, her face wrinkling at its heat. I held it there, waiting, until she had drunk some more of it.

"What time did you and Joey go to the party?" I asked.

She turned her head slowly and looked at me as if she were seeing me for the first time. I didn't believe she was that far gone.

"Come on, Stella. I have to know these things. If you don't tell me, you'll have to tell the police."

She managed to lift her own cup this time.

"What time did you and Joey go to the party?"

"I met him there—" she said. I could barely hear her. "I had to go home and dress—about eight o'clock."

"Where else did you go—before that?"

"Right here. I was here. You remember."

"All the time, Stella, until you went home to dress?"

"Yes. I waited for Joey to dress. After Francie went to work."

Francie's lip curled slightly. She had turned from me to watch Stella.

"I got to the party at nine-thirty," I said. "You'd been there an hour and a half. Is that right?"

"Yes."

"And you gave Joey the shot of heroin around eight-thirty or nine o'clock. Is that right?"

She was looking down at the table now. Francie had lowered her hands slowly till they lay stretched flat on the table top. Her eyes bored into Stella's face.

Stella nodded weakly.

"You—" Francie half rose and I motioned to her to sit down again.

"And you didn't see Bill Denton at any time during the evening?"

"No."

"You didn't know he was there?"

She shook her head.

"You didn't hear anybody bring him in there?"

"No."

"So you didn't know Bill Denton was dead on the floor in the next room until I showed you?"

She sat there with her head hanging. Francie's eyes swung, as if they had been suspended on a long cord, slowly, almost imperceptibly, till they were looking into mine. I looked back at her and I told her about it and she sat with her head on her hand, watching me tell her, without interruption, until I had finished. Then she got up and looked out the one small window behind the table.

"And you brought Joey here," she said.

"Yeah."

"And then you called the cops. After that."

"That's right."

There was a period of silence. Then she turned from the window and looked at me levelly across the table.

"I guess I had you figured wrong, Mr. Donnelly."

"All right, Francie," I said. "Would you like to leave me alone with Stella for a few minutes?"

"If you think it's safe."

It was a grim attempt, but it was an attempt and I tried to smile a thank you. I don't know whether I made it or not. My face was stiff and not like my own face at all.

Francie picked up her cup, filled it again with the powdered coffee and hot water and went out of the kitchen. I drank some more of my own, put the cup down and tapped Stella's shoulder.

"Let's talk it over," I said. "We're alone now."

She lifted her head and looked at me with a totally tragic expression. But her eyes were dry.

The kitchen was small and unventilated and the heat from the stove had made it stifling. I took off my coat and hung it over the back of my chair.

"Do you know how much trouble you may be in, Stella?" I said. "And Joey too?"

"I know."

"Maybe I can help you. But you'll have to talk to me."

I was standing beside her chair. Her tortured little face turned up. Suddenly she grabbed at my arms and fell forward against me. She buried her face in my chest and hung on, her hands pulling at my shirtsleeves.

"Oh—Mr. Donnelly!" she wailed.

I let her hang on for a minute, hoping she wasn't rubbing all her lipstick off on my shirt. Then I pushed her back in the chair till she had to look at me.

"Please—" I said.

Her face changed, grew dark and stormy.

"All my life people yelled at me. My mother, my father, my teachers. They beat me too! My mother used to beat me with a strap."

She stopped talking suddenly and studied my face. Then she came slowly up out of the chair.

"You don't believe it, do you? You don't believe she beat me. All right, I'll show you!"

She grabbed the hem of her skirt and pulled up on it. I caught both of her hands, loosened them, curled her fingers into fists and replaced them at her side.

"I'll take your word for it, Stella. What's the pitch? Let's have the whole thing."

She pouted.

"Don't believe me. I don't care. You think I'm just a crazy—bobby soxer or something. Maybe worse." She raised her voice a notch. "A juvenile delinquent! That's what you think I am!"

"Take it easy, Stella," I said. "Have I been yelling at you?"

Her eyes finally managed to fill with tears. She sank back into the chair again.

"I don't like to drink," she said. "I only drank tonight because they made me, the other kids. I didn't want to give Joey that shot. He forced me to do it. I don't belong with them." She glanced at the kitchen door and lowered her voice. "I'm not really in love with Joey even."

I kept quiet.

"I'm in love with somebody else."

"Well, all right—"

"Mr. Donnelly—you're not like the others. You're different—a grown man—mature. Not like Joey and those wild kids."

She reached for me again and I stepped back out of the way. She caught her balance and stayed where she was.

"Will you help me, please? I know it's wrong to fall in love with you. I shouldn't tell you—But I can't help it. I've been keeping it shut up inside —"

"Stop it, Stella," I said. "You're not in love with me. We have other things to talk about, remember?"

She turned from me slowly, straightened her shoulders and stared into space. Just like in the movies.

"I didn't think you'd be—cruel," she said. "I thought at least you'd understand—"

"I understand some things," I said. "I understand that Bill Denton is dead, and you were there, on the other side of a thin wall, and you've been talking about everything else in the world for five minutes—"

She wheeled and gave me the tortured look.

"All right!" she said. "Beat me. Like the others. You might as well. Go ahead. Shall I get a strap—?"

The door swung open and it was Francie. She looked scared.

"The doctor wants you," she said.

I left Stella and joined Francie at the door. It closed behind us and I went through the open door of Joey's bedroom. It was dark in there except for the light from the living room. Dr. Stein was standing beside the bed and Joey was sitting straight up in it. Francie came in behind me and I felt her fingers clutch stiffly at my arm.

Dr. Stein beckoned me to the bed and Joey stared up at me, his mouth working.

"Hi, Joey," I said. "How does your head feel?"

"O.K.," he said dully.

"Can you see me all right?"

"Yeh, yeh. I can see you."

"You know who I am?"

He gazed at me.

"Louis?"

"No," I said. "Donnelly. The coach."

He seemed to think it over.

"Where's Francie?" he said.

"Right here, Joey."

"Francie—" She moved out around me and went to the bed.

"Yeah, Joey," she said.

"Francie, I got to get up. Got to contact Mr. Smith—" She looked quickly over her shoulder at me.

"Who's Mr. Smith, Joey?" I asked.

He looked at me with suspicion.

"You ain't Louis," he said.

"No. I'm Donnelly. The coach."

"What you want with me?"

Francie was patting his arm gently, trying to soothe him.

"Lie down, Joey," she said. "They're here to help you."

He pushed back the bedclothes and got both feet on the floor. Then he drooped forward, catching his head with his hands.

"If you get up now, Joey," I said, "you'll run into cops. They'll pick you up, ask questions."

The word came, muffled and dull between his fingers.

"Cops?"

"That's right. Will you do me a favor? Get back in bed and wait till tomorrow."

"Got to—get—Mr. Smith—" I tried again.

"Who's Mr. Smith? Maybe I could call him for you."

He lifted his head and the suspicion had turned to cunning.

"You never heard of Mr. Smith, did you?"

"Yes, Joey. I heard of him."

Dr. Stein had a box of white pills in his hand. He took Joey's hand, held it up and dropped a pill into it.

"Here's something to help you sleep," he said.

"What is it?"

"Codeine. It's something like morphine."

He turned the pill in his fingers.

"Dope, huh?"

"Yes, Joey."

"How d'you take it? You got to cook it first?"

"No. You just swallow it."

After a while he put it on his tongue and swallowed it. But he continued to sit with his feet on the floor.

Then suddenly again he was struggling to get on his feet and I grabbed his arms to steady him. He looked squarely into my face for about half a minute, then sank down again, trembling. I looked at Stein.

"Can I ask him a question?" I said.

He nodded.

"Joey—try to remember—did you go anywhere else besides the party tonight?"

"Mr. Smith," he muttered. "Got to contact Mr. Smith."

"Who is Mr. Smith, Joey?"

He didn't even try to answer. He muttered some more, but the words, if they were words, didn't make sense. He dropped back onto the pillow and I lifted his legs and got them covered. Dr. Stein got his bag shut and followed Francie and me into the living room.

"Will he be all right?" Francie asked.

Dr. Stein took off his glasses, found a cloth in his pocket and sat there cleaning them.

"I don't know. He should be in a hospital. They have the machines—"

"At fifty dollars a day," Francie said.

Dr. Stein was silent. I remembered Stella and went back to the kitchen. I might have saved the steps. Stella was gone.

CHAPTER NINE

I got into my coat and went back to the living room. Dr. Stein was handing Francie the box of codeine pills and a slip of white paper.

"To help him sleep," he said. "You may take one yourself, Miss, if you need it."

"That's a funny thing," Francie said with some bitterness. "Get it from a doctor and it's O.K. Find it for yourself, it's a crime."

"It has to be that way," Dr. Stein said patiently.

"How about all those doctors they catch selling it to bums?"

"Sometimes," he nodded. "Sometimes yes. There should be a place where a man—woman—an addict could go for help. Such a place there should be."

"There's always jail," she said.

"We don't want Joey to go to jail," Dr. Stein said.

Francie had had a stomach full of confusion. She tossed the paper and the pills onto a chair and looked first at one, then the other of us, her hands on her hips, her eyes spitting fire.

"I wish somebody would explain to me," she said, "what the hell is going on! All this special stuff! For Joey Arvin. People like us don't get things for free. It's fishy. It smells funny. Let me in on it, please. The next thing I know, you'll have the Chief of Police down here, apologizing."

I had had my round with her earlier and now left it up to the doctor. He had more equipment in the head. He had to have.

"Miss Arvin," he said patiently, "it may well be that we will have not only the Chief of Police, but the Mayor and the District Attorney too. You must not be alarmed in advance. Nothing has happened tomorrow. We are trying to help not only your Joey, but all the others too. In a new way. In a scientific way. You can help."

"Oh sure—"

"You can help by trying to keep your head and by trusting us. We can't promise you nothing will happen to Joey. But we try—we try hard to work things out so everybody gets—what is it?—a fair deal."

The steam had gone from Francie again, but her suspicion remained. She turned away wearily.

60

"So run for president," she said. "You don't tell me anything. Big talk. I heard more big talk in my life than in the entire history of the world."

Dr. Stein looked at me blankly and picked up his bag.

"I go now to see Dr. Clark," he said.

"What about Joey?" I asked.

"Somebody should stay by him. I left a statement—if the police come, he's not to be disturbed."

"Thanks for coming, Doctor," I said.

He shrugged massively and shifted his bag to the other hand.

"So good," he said. "If Joey wakes up in pain he should have one of the pills. One every three hours if he wants. If he complains of blindness, you should immediately call the city hospital and send him. We will try to make some financial arrangements."

He started out, then turned back and looked at Francie out of his big face.

"Remember what I said," he said. "Nothing has happened tomorrow. If everybody works together, in time we cure the whole world."

He went out. Pretty soon Francie said, "Did he mean that? Or is he a crazy, mixed-up kid too?"

"He meant it all right. If it were up to him alone—"

"One guy alone—in a world like this?"

"Yeah," I said. "Silly thought, isn't it?"

There was some silence. I knew I had to get going, but to leave her suddenly would be to walk out on her.

"Did Stella sneak out on you?" she said.

"Yeah."

"Uh-huh," she said wisely.

"You know where she lives?"

She told me. Her face twisted with anger.

"That Stella! I tell him and tell him she's no good. Giving him that stuff—"

"Do many of the others use it—friends of Joey's?"

"Sure, plenty of them. The only reason I let Joey go out for the ball team—I thought it might help him stay away from it."

"If we catch it now, before it gets hold of him—" She couldn't hear me.

"It killed his father and mother," she said. "They were both junkies. I used to come home from school and they'd be in bed, the two of them, sleeping off a jag. I used to cook and shop and clean the house—all of it, all the time. After school I had a job and the money I got went to the old man for more junk because he would get on his knees and beg me for it. I

61

would have been on the stuff myself, only I never got around to it. I never had the time."

I tried to shift the subject out of the past.

"How much do you make on your job?" I asked her.

"Depending on how much I put up with—maybe forty, fifty dollars a week."

"You're a pretty girl, Francie. You have experience. Why not get a better job? In another part of town?"

"You're some joker."

"It could be done. There are other neighborhoods. You and Joey could both get a better break."

Her face seemed to be thinking it over, but not for long.

"There's Louis," she said. "He'd never let me move."

"Louis's grown up. I don't see that he's your problem."

"He's my brother."

"But if you laid down the law—you pay the bills—"

"Louis wouldn't go. In this neighborhood he's a big shot. Somewhere else, he'd be a nobody. Louis couldn't stand that."

"And you have to take care of Louis—a twenty-five-year-old man—"

"He's my brother. Somebody has to take care of him. You know anybody else?"

Offhand I didn't.

Somebody knocked on the door and Francie went to open it. Outside in the hall were two cops. They came on in.

They were ordinary, run-of-the-mill, footsore plain-clothesmen, wanting to talk to Joey Arvin. Francie kept quiet. I explained to them that Joey was not to be disturbed. One of them, the one who did the talking, looked me over briefly and said, "Who are you?"

I showed him my ID card and he read it and gave it to his partner to read. The partner handed it back to me.

"How come you're here?" the first one asked.

I explained that I had visited Joey earlier in the day and had brought a doctor to look at him tonight. The doctor's name was Stein and they could check on him clear up to City Hall.

The talking cop was a man of forty-five, built stocky with some paunch. Evidently he had been on duty for several shifts, because he needed a shave, his suit needed pressing and his eyes were bloodshot and bleary. He looked at me some more, then rubbed his eyes with the palms of his hands. When he looked up again, his face had cleared some.

"Could we take a look at the kid?" he said. "Make sure he's in there?"

"Certainly," I said. "I'd appreciate it if you wouldn't wake him up."

"We'll take off our shoes," he said.

Very funny man. If he took them off now, he'd never get them back on.

I led them to Joey's door, opened it and they stepped inside quietly. Joey was lying on his right side, asleep. They peered at him in the half dark, then backed out of the room and I closed the door. The cop rubbed his eyes again.

"When you think we could talk to him?" he said.

"I don't know. You'd have to get in touch with Dr. Stein."

"Where would we do that?"

"He works for the Board of Education. You could find out through City Hall."

He looked for a while at the whisky bottle Louis had left on the table.

"You been here all evening?" he asked me.

"No. Just for the last hour."

He looked at Francie.

"This is Francine Arvin," I said, "Joey's sister."

The cop nodded.

"Louis at home?" he said.

Francie nodded.

"Was Joey home all evening?" he asked her.

Francie looked him in the eye.

"I don't know. I was at work."

I could see him trying to work on it, but he was very tired. He rubbed his eyes some more, gathered his shoulders in a kind of hopeless shrug and said, "O.K. We'll see the kid later."

At the door he turned and looked back at me.

"I seen you somewhere," he said.

"Maybe at one of the ball games," I said.

He shook his head slowly.

"I never went to a high school ball game. Somewhere else."

I moved toward the door. He kept looking at me and I let him look. Then he shrugged and opened the door.

"I'll think of it," he said. "Good night, Miss Arvin."

They went out and walked heavily down the stairs. I picked up my hat.

"Where are you going?" she asked.

It startled me. It wasn't Francie's kind of question.

"I've got a few errands," I said. "Are you nervous about staying alone? Did you want me to do something more?"

She looked away.

"No. Thanks for everything."

"It's all right. You better get some sleep."

Her mouth twisted grimly.

"My beauty sleep?"

63

"I meant it, Francie."

I had my hand on the doorknob. She came across the room and stood close to me, but without touching me.

"Thanks again," she said. "Thanks for saying I'm—pretty."

I got the door open.

"You asked me," she said, "about—Mr. Smith."

"Yes."

She wouldn't look at me now. She spoke low and rapidly, as if afraid I might interrupt her.

"There's a Mr. Smith—I don't know who he is. He's a big shot. He runs most everything, especially people like us. I never saw him. Nobody I know ever saw him."

"Is he a real man, Francie? Or just a name?"

She looked at me then, frank and open, straight into my face.

"He's a real man," she said.

I touched her arm lightly. She raised her hand and brushed it across mine, then dropped it quickly.

"Good night, Francie," I said. "Try to get some sleep."

Her touch stayed with me all the way downstairs and into the street.

CHAPTER TEN

The place where the party had been had the hollow, still-quivering look of a suddenly evacuated room. The colored lights in the floor lamps were still burning. Some strips of the colored paper had torn loose and hung crazily at odd angles from the ceiling. A couple of the sofas that lined the walls had been displaced and stood crudely out of line. The floor was littered and you could see now on the old, dry wood the stains and rough spots that had come with the years and never been cleaned or touched up. The smell of the bodies lingered in the stale air, along with cheap perfumes and shaving lotions, and on a splinter in the doorjamb hung a fragment of red cloth, torn from a girl's dress.

I stood in the doorway at the bottom of the steps and thought, I wonder where they all went?

The two doors in the rear wall were closed. I stepped inside and started toward the door to the bedroom where I had found Joey and Stella. Halfway across the floor I stopped. There was bright light showing under the door and there were sounds beyond it, hard, brittle sounds of voices and feet.

I went back to the street, walked to the alley and looked toward the rear of the building. A black-and-white squad car was parked opposite the back door and a light shone brightly from the vestibule where I had seen the trash cans. A patrolman in uniform was wandering idly in the alley near the car, kicking at scraps of debris.

It wouldn't do any good to go back there now. Maybe later. But later, the cops would have picked up whatever there was that seemed important, and if there was anything they had missed, it would have been scuffed, mauled, tossed or smeared into uselessness. Still, it would be wise to have a look later.

It was nearly midnight and the air had grown colder. I walked rapidly over the now familiar route, toward the saloon where Francie worked. There was little traffic on the street and I saw practically no pedestrians. I had expected to run into knots of kids, hanging around after the party or waiting to resume it. But I saw none.

The party at the saloon was still going strong and I crossed the nearly deserted street catty-corner, heading for the door of the joint. It opened as

I approached and I got there in time to meet my silver-haired lady again, face to face. I had been hurrying and I reached for the knob before she had let go of it. She let go quickly and our hands brushed together. I let the door swing shut.

"I beg your pardon," she said softly, stepping out of the way.

She had a voice like the middle tones of a cello.

I touched my hat. We looked at each other for a moment and I thought I ought to say something, but I couldn't think of anything to say. I reached for the door again, pulled it open and went in. I looked back at her once and she was standing in the entryway, gazing into the street.

The place was crowded now and I had to push my way to the back where the telephone hung behind the jukebox. I found out then where some, at least, of the kids from the party had wound up. They were two deep at the bar and all the booths and tables were occupied. In one booth there were eight of them, the girls sitting on the boys' laps.

I had to look up Cameron's number again and this time I made a mental note of the address. I dialed the number and the line was busy. I waited, staying by the phone, and dialed again. Still busy. I checked the address once more and decided the hell with telephones.

I shouldered my way back through the crowds toward the door. At the front between the end of the bar and the street window was a small space still unjammed by customers. Doubtless there was no service in that area. There were two men standing there and they weren't drinking. One of them was my fat friend, Beasly. The other I had never seen.

I held to my route. Beasly had not been looking at me and I thought I could get out before he would see me. But the crowd in the first booth surged into the aisle, holding me up, and by the time I reached the door, Beasly was in front of it with his big belly between me and freedom.

He took the dead cigar out of his mouth and gave me one of those smiles. His companion stood apart, showing no interest. He was a slight, tightly-built guy in a well-cut gray suit, wearing an expensive gray hat, immaculate hands and face and a total, long-practiced deadpan.

"Yeah Beasly," I said. "If you'll excuse me—" I reached for the door-knob, but somehow he got his fat bulk in the way.

"We seem to keep bumping into each other, Coach," he said.

"We do at that."

He looked at the end of his cigar with some regret, then stuck it back in his mouth.

"You evidently don't keep training rules, the way you tell the kids, eh? It's pretty late."

I glanced over my shoulder.

"Evidently the kids don't keep them either," I said.

He shrugged. It made him shake all over.

"Well, you know kids. Everybody's got to live a little."

"You are so right," I said. "And it's not always easy, is it?"

He took the cigar out and studied it some more. I kept wishing I knew what the hell we were sparring about. I looked past his shoulder and saw the Duchess, walking with dignity and poise toward the curb, where a cab had drawn up. She'd probably caught the last one in the neighborhood. I could walk to Riverside Drive.

"Coach," Beasly was saying, "I thought you might be able to help us— I can't seem to locate Joey Arvin."

"Have you tried real hard?"

"It worries me," he said. "Joey was kind of a sick boy, and we wouldn't want to see anything happen to him, would we, Coach?"

I stared at him.

"Is that all you had on your mind, Beasly?"

His eyebrows lifted.

"A—yeah, that's all."

"All right. The last I heard, about fifteen minutes ago, Joey Arvin was sound asleep in his own bed in his own house and his sister Francie was taking care of him. Now, if you'll excuse me—" But he didn't move. He glanced at his companion, but I couldn't see that the little gray man gave him much help. I decided that if Beasly didn't move out of the way by the time I could count to three and a half, I would push him.

He must have read my mind, because he shifted, settling back against the glass door. It would be hard to push him from that position.

"Oh—well then," he said. "Sorry I held you up, Coach. Let's have a drink together—you know—no hard feelings?"

"I've got no time for a drink," I said. "If you'll excuse me—" I turned from him and bumped into the little man in the gray suit. He had a hand inside his coat, just resting there in a kind of Napoleonic pose. I could tell he was used to it. I could tell he had been in the business a long time.

"All right," I said, "order it up. Is it on me?"

Beasly put a pudgy hand on my arm.

"Oh no, Coach!" he said. "It's on me."

We shouldered our way toward the bar. It took a long time. The press was heavy. Beasly ran interference. I followed him and the gray man came along, close behind me. I couldn't figure it out for several minutes, and then it began to trickle through, part of it—the old routine. Delay. Tie the guy up and slow him down.

But why?

Beasly finally got the bartender's eye and he came up with three high-balls. They weren't very good. I guessed he had forgotten I was a friend of Francie's.

I tried to hurry through it, but Beasly and the gray man were taking their time and they had me blocked well in against the bar, with those milling kids all around. It was no good place to start a fight that I would no doubt lose anyway.

Nobody made any conversation. We just stood there, drinking, staring at one another. It began to get under my skin. I wondered how far the Duchess had got in the cab.

There was a sudden break in the crowd of kids and I set my glass down on the bar and started through it. The gray man got in the way.

"Have another one, Coach," he said.

"No."

He glanced at Beasly.

"Don't want to detain you," the fat man said. "Thought we might have a friendly drink. But if you have to go—"

"I have to go," I said.

They glanced at each other again and I saw the fat one shrug slightly. The gray man glided out of my way.

"Good night, Coach," Beasly called.

"Yeah," I said.

I'd spent at least twenty minutes fooling around with them and all I'd got for it was a lousy drink and a hot feeling around the eyeballs. When I hit the fresh air, it felt like a cold shower after a fast game of handball.

I stopped in the glow of light through the door and pulled Beasly's card out of my pocket. It read:

HERMAN BEASLY—FINE USED CARS

In the lower right corner, in smaller print, it read:

Car rentals—U-drive

There was a telephone number and an address in this neighborhood.

I put the card away and headed for the curb. There was a click of high heels and I glanced at the girl walking toward the saloon. She paid no attention to me, but turned toward the door. I caught a flash of the faded blue uniform.

"Francie—" I said.

She stopped and waited, rigid at the door.

"What about Joey?" I said.

"He's all right. Louis's there."

"I don't get it. You heard what Dr. Stein said."

She looked at me flatly, emptily.

"I hate cops," she said. "All cops. All kinds of cops—public and private."

68

She twisted the knob of the door and pushed into the joint.

So that made it all quite clear. I wondered when and how she'd found out. Remembering the short time that had passed, I could think of only one answer. Louis had told her.

How had Louis found out? From Beasly?

How had Beasly found out?

Maybe that cop who'd thought he'd seen me before—he seemed to know everybody in the neighborhood.

No matter how—Louis could only be a messenger boy.

For whom?

I walked down the street in the dark, looking for a cab.

CHAPTER ELEVEN

It was late to go calling, but it was a call that had to be made. They weren't paying me to keep regular hours. Come to think of it, they weren't paying me to investigate killings either.

I thought about that while I waited at the front door of a wide, Colonial house in the Riverside Drive section—a part of the city I had never seen before. It didn't matter really. They were paying me enough. If death was part of the job, I was stuck with it.

The door opened suddenly and I almost fell inside. The guy looking out at me was tall, stringy and weathered—old family retainer type. He looked miserable. I imagined he would always look miserable.

I asked to see Cameron and he told me to wait and shut the door in my face. I waited. I had decided he would never return, was about to lean on the bell some more, when the door opened again and he nodded me inside. I crossed a wide reception hall, went through a set of French doors. Beyond was a combination library and den that ran half the width of the house. The woodwork was dark and heavy. There were bookshelves on three walls and in the fourth, a fireplace with a low fire burning in it.

David Cameron sat in a high-backed, leather swivel chair behind a huge mahogany desk. He was still impressive, in spite of his small size, in spite of his tired, preoccupied expression. He lacked some of that alertness he'd shown that first time I'd met him, in the D.A.'s office, but he was still plenty impressive.

I balanced my hat on my knee, leaned forward in the chair beside the desk and got down to business. There was no point in our playing with each other. If he was still against me, I'd find out soon enough, and if he could help me any with the problem of Bill Denton, that would be worth something.

"It's about a kid named Bill Denton," I said. "Were you acquainted with him?"

He nodded wearily.

"Very well. I am his godfather."

My hat slid sideways on my knee and I straightened it up.

"He's dead," I said. "Somebody killed him."

"We've been friends of his family for years—" He jerked his white head around to stare at me. "He's what?"

"He was killed—some time tonight. I found this note on him."

I found the scrap of paper from Bill's pocket and handed it to him across the corner of the desk. It took some time for him to smooth it out and get his eyes focused on it. He read it silently. After he'd finished, he pushed it back to me, ran his thin hands through that white hair and sank back in his chair.

"I'm glad to have seen it," he said, "but you may be in trouble with the police. Wouldn't this constitute evidence?"

"I figure I'm part of the police for the time being. Also, you'll pardon me for saying, I wasn't sure how I stood with you and I thought that if the cops should come to you and everybody would get to talking. the first thing you know—" He smiled faintly, nodding.

"It would get into the papers," he said.

"That's right."

His smile faded slowly.

"You're a careful and clever man," he said. "It's true, I tried to dissuade the city from hiring you in the beginning. But once the decision was made, I was willing to forget about it. I would never have given you away."

I cleared my throat.

"I believe it," I said.

"About the boy, Bill—I can't believe it. Why? Why would it happen to him?"

"I don't know. There were rumors that a young hood named Louis Arvin was out to get him, because Arvin's young brother had got beaned by a baseball. Bill Denton was the one who threw the ball."

"Ridiculous. Youngsters don't kill for such reasons—"

"Louis Arvin is no youngster. But I think you're probably right. I came here to show you this letter and to ask whether you'd been in touch with Bill Denton during the past twelve hours."

"No," he said, "I haven't seen Bill for several weeks. We used to see a lot of each other. This letter you found would indicate he had something heavy on his mind. But he never finished the letter. If he had—"

"If he had," I agreed. I picked up my hat, stuck the letter back in my pocket. "I won't keep you any longer. I'll turn this over to the D. A now that you've seen it."

The telephone rang. I was on my feet and when he didn't pick it up right away, I started to back away. He gestured to me to wait. He picked up the phone, identified himself and listened. I could hear the scratch of a man's voice on the other end, but couldn't make out any words. Cameron glanced at me once, then began to slump in his chair. He had the look of a man who'd been taking a steady beating for a long time. Finally he said:

"Thank you for calling. Keep looking. She must be somewhere in the city."

He hung up, passed his hand across his forehead and worked up another of those painful, grim smiles.

"Excuse the interruption," he said.

"I'll be going," I said. "May I use the telephone?" He indicated the phone at his elbow and I went around there and picked it up. Dialing Austin Clark's number, I found myself staring at a chrome-framed photograph on an easel in the far corner of the desk. It was a photograph of a woman and I had no trouble at all recognizing her. The picture was inscribed: "To David with love—Marian." She was my Duchess with the silver hair. She was wearing a casual white blouse with a row of pearl buttons down the front. None of the buttons was missing.

A woman answered the phone at Clark's end. I told her who I was.

"This is Mrs. Clark," she said. "Austin told me to tell you that he would be in the District Attorney's office. He'd like you to meet him there."

I thanked her and hung up. I was still staring at the picture of the Duchess and Cameron noticed it "Maybe," he said, "I haven't shown proper concern over the tragedy of Bill Denton. I assure you, I'm horribly shocked. But at the moment, I have a personal problem—" I nodded at the picture.

"Your wife?" I said.

"She's—somewhat neurotic. From time to time, she runs away. Maybe you can understand. It's hard to think about anything else. I've been sitting here by the phone all evening—"

"I'm sorry."

"I'm sure she'll turn up," he said. "You have my complete confidence and cooperation. Call on me any time."

I went out then and down the front walk toward the cab waiting for me at the curb. I didn't know what it meant to be a godfather and I'd never had any kids of my own. But I could imagine that a dead godson, combined with a wife that ran away every so often and you had to hire a private eye to find her—that combination could probably get under a man's skin. I couldn't hold it against him that he hadn't gone into a coma when I told him about Bill Denton.

I climbed into the cab and asked him to take me to City Hall. He did it efficiently and quietly.

Clark was waiting for me in the D.A.'s private office. The D.A. had the look in his eyes of a man who had been kicked in the stomach every few minutes for the last five hours. It was now shortly after 1:00 a.m. If Clark had the jitters he didn't show it. He was on his full dignity and very calm. I couldn't see how he'd managed it, because he must have had to sit there quite a while in silence. The D.A. was busy with some papers and they had not been talking when I entered. I gathered he'd made Clark wait for me.

I found a chair, we exchanged looks and then we both waited some more. After a couple of ages, the D.A. looked up and started to talk.

"I was with Mayor Towne from eleven o'clock until midnight," he said. "From midnight till a few minutes ago, I was with Mr. Clarence Denton, the father of the boy who was killed. Now I am with you." He paused with considerable effect. "Gentlemen, I trust you can help me."

"In any way we can," Clark said.

"To put it as mildly as I can," the D.A. said, "the Mayor is extremely disturbed. I myself am disturbed. Young Denton's father is nearly beside himself and the Chief of Police is dangerously puzzled."

"I'm sorry—" Clark started.

The D.A. held up his hand. I saw it was shaking slightly.

"Before you get sorrier," he said, "let me tell you where we are sitting. Six months ago, a girl of six was killed and her body stuffed in a trash can, not three blocks from the scene of Bill Denton's murder. This crime has not been solved, but its investigation continued, week after week— until six weeks ago."

Clark shifted quietly in his chair, but his face showed nothing.

"At that time, Dr. Clark, you managed to sell the Mayor, the Chief of Police and—unfortunately—me, an idea. A new approach to what we eu-phemistically call 'juvenile delinquency.' I don't have to go into the de-tails. But the kernel of the idea involved a professional—detective—who would win the confidence of the tougher elements among your students and would follow through to help us clean up the case of the murdered girl and initiate some kind of recreation program—or something—to keep things smoothed out."

Clark shifted again and opened his mouth, but the D.A. waved him down.

"I know, there were other considerations, high and noble aims, worthy objectives, impeccable goals. We can discuss them some other time."

He swung suddenly in his chair, his arm shot out and his finger pointed straight at me.

"You, sir, were that professional—detective."

I'll bet he's hell on wheels in a courtroom, I thought.

I nodded and he settled back again.

73

"Let me make it clear," he said more calmly, "that I respect Dr. Stein as a physician; I respect you, Dr. Clark, as an educator and—" he swung around to me again, "I have heard of your reputation as an honest private investigator who, through luck or unusual skill, has been of some assistance to the Chicago police."

His next pause was amply dramatic.

"But let me also make it clear, gentlemen, that as of one o'clock this morning, you have managed to unsell me on your fancy plan totally, thoroughly and irrevocably. Unfortunately, you have not yet unsold the Mayor nor, I understand, the Board of Education. We're in a kind of stalemate. This can't go on very long."

He paused again. The axe was high in the air—right over me.

"I want all the cards on the table," he said slowly. "I tell you now—if, through your methods, the murder of the little girl, and the murder of young Denton are not wrapped up to my satisfaction within the next forty-eight hours, I will press for an abrogation of your contract with this city. If you wish to sue for breach, that is up to you. I doubt that you can win."

I kept quiet.

"The reason I doubt that you can win is because there is a clause in that contract which provides that during its life, there will be no interference with established police methods in criminal investigation without the express consent of the District Attorney."

He was looking hard at me. Clark spoke up quickly.

"Are you saying—?" he started.

The D.A. ploughed on.

"Last night," he said, "somebody did some rearranging of personnel at the scene of the discovery of young Denton's body."

"But—" Clark said.

I stood up. I couldn't let him carry the whole thing. It had become everybody's baby; everybody's big, brawling, fat, incorrigible baby.

"All right," I said. "I took a boy named Joey Arvin out of a bedroom in that apartment to his home, because he was in need of medical attention. I took his girl friend along because I thought I might need some help with him."

"You knew in advance he needed medical attention? I understood the doctor didn't see him till later."

I ignored that.

"About the contract," I said, "if it's a question of my efficiency or qualifications, then I'll resign. If it's a question of choosing between Dr. Clark's plan and routine police methods—then I'll string along with Clark. But I tell you this: I did not undertake under that contract to solve a specific murder and I would not undertake now to solve still another murder within forty-eight hours and if the contract hangs on that, then I'm through. I'll go quietly."

He stared hard at me, then waved his hand.

"Sit down," he said.

I stayed on my feet. The D.A. ran a big hand over his face and when he spoke again his voice had that exaggerated patience of a man who's fighting to hold himself in.

"Let's face a few facts," he said. "I know there are links between juvenile and adult crime. I know there's an organized ring operating in the city. According to our estimates the total value of the standard merchandise involved in criminal activity—hot cars, stolen furs, narcotics—for the last year alone was five million dollars. In a city this size, that's a lot; that's a whole hell of a lot and you couldn't round that much up without an organization."

"There is an organization," I said. "It's run by one man. They call him 'Mr. Smith.'"

He gaped at me.

"That's fantastic," he said. "It couldn't be a one-man operation. It's too big."

"Not if he's smart enough and big enough and has enough kids working for him."

He waved me down again. He had decided it was ridiculous. He turned to Clark.

"So all your motives, Dr. Clark, and most of your reasoning, are laudable. But I know this—as District Attorney of this county, forty-eight hours is as long as I can hold back the newspapers, the rank and file cops and the armchair reformers. Maybe not even that long."

Clark tried to say something and got waved down again. The D.A. was great with the waving down. When he wanted the floor, he took it.

"Mr. Clarence Denton," he said, "is a respected, peaceable man, living in a modest home on a quiet street. He finds it hard to understand how a thing like that could happen to his boy and still harder to understand how we can ask him to keep still about it and not speak to the reporters. He has the feeling that if such things can happen, it ought to be in the papers. People ought to know." Clark's face had begun to show some strain.

"But it's always got into the papers and it never helped," he said. "You get a swirl of emotion, you get headlines for a week about the drive on teen-age hoodlums, and then the story dies out and the readers imagine that some wild kids did a bad thing and the police will deal with them and that's the end, until the next outbreak. This gets us nowhere! We're closer to the basic facts now than ever before. A little more time—" The D.A. laid his hands carefully, flatly on the desk.

"Time, Dr. Clark," he said, "is what we no longer have any of."

A buzzer sounded faintly and he broke off to flip a switch on his intercom. A girl spoke into it and the D.A. said,

"Yes, Miss Allison. Bring it in, please."

A tired-looking, middle-aged woman came in, carrying a manila envelope, sealed with brown tape. There was a note on it in pencil. The D.A. glanced at it and pushed it to one side. I was relieved. If they were pictures of Bill Denton, I didn't want to see them.

Clark got up and nodded to me. The D.A. swung around in his big chair and looked at us.

"The only advice I can give you," he said, "is to climb on the ball and for God's sake keep it rolling. Otherwise, this office, this administration and this political party will go into a long, dark eclipse."

"There are some questions I'd like to ask Mr. Denton," I said.

"I have a full statement from Mr. Denton," the D.A. said, "covering all the known movements of the boy from the time he got home from school until he disappeared from the house. Will that do?"

There wasn't much I could say.

"If I could have a copy—" I said.

He pushed the buzzer and we waited till Miss Allison came in again. The D.A. told her what we wanted. She went out and came back with a thin sheaf of white paper with typewriting on it. She gave it to the D.A., the D.A. gave it to me and I folded it and put it in my pocket. Clark started toward the office door, but the D.A. stopped him.

"Better go out the other way," he said. "There are newshawks in the corridor."

We reversed direction and headed for the private exit. There were two doors, one reading IN and the other OUT. I reached to push the OUT door and the other one opened. There was a man standing in it, Clarence Denton, Bill's father. We had met a couple of times, at ball games at the school. He was a nice, friendly kind of guy with some kind of small manufacturing business. We looked at each other and I couldn't bring myself to ignore him. His dead boy was in his face and death in a living face is hard to look at.

"Hello, Donnelly," he said, nodding uncertainly. "Dr. Clark—" I couldn't think of anything to say. Clark came through as usual.

Denton waved his hand vaguely and went on into the office. The D.A. spoke suddenly.

"One more thing, Clark," he said. "I'm going to call Dave Cameron in on this. It's time he knew about it. We need him."

"No!" Denton said.

I looked back and the D.A. was staring at Denton.

76

"I called him—" Denton said, "just now—while I was waiting. Told him about Bill. This isn't the time. He has—his own problems."

The D.A. looked at him as if he understood completely.

"Marian again?" he said.

It was as if Clark and I had left. But I stayed.

"…Sitting there all evening by the phone…" Denton said.

Clark touched my arm. I followed him out the door and into the private, automatic elevator. Going down, Clark stood with his hat in his hand, staring at the floor.

"There are a thousand kids in the school," he said. "I've met the parents of maybe three hundred of them, one time or another. Most of them are people like Denton. The others, the parents or relatives of the Joey Arvins, the Stella Perinos, I've never seen. As far as I know, they don't even exist."

I became aware that he had stopped talking.

"Yeah," I said.

We got out of the elevator and walked into the City Hall parking lot, where he had left his car.

"What about the ball game?" I asked.

"I've already called the other school for a cancellation. I thought—you might be busy."

"I might at that."

"Let me give you a ride home."

"I've got a stop to make," I said. "I'll report in tomorrow."

He studied me briefly, then climbed into his car.

"Be careful, Mac," he said. "We need you. We need you badly."

"Good night," I said.

He drove away and I walked back through the parking lot to the street in front of the City Hall. It was deserted, but there was a phone box on a post near the curb and I yanked on the gadget till some operator came up with a sleepy hello. I asked for a cab and she said there'd be one along in a minute. I hung up the phone and leaned against the post, waiting. Far down the block, a taxi pulled out from the curb and drifted slowly toward me. I stepped to the curb, but it drifted on by. There had been a passenger in the rear seat. It looked like a woman, but I couldn't see her face.

I waited some more and a cab pulled in and I got into the back seat. I gave him the address of the party apartment on Grand near Fourteenth. He was no more talkative than the previous driver and I fell asleep during the ride.

CHAPTER TWELVE

The front door had been closed now and locked, and looking through the one small front window, I saw that the lights had been turned off. The sagging strips of colored paper were gray wisps in the gloom. I climbed the steps and went around to the alley. The squad car was gone and there were no more lights or sounds from the rear. I walked back there and tried the service door. It was locked, but it hung loosely and the jamb was rotten and if the knob would hold, I could open it all right. I felt through a pile of rubbish near the door and found a broken tire iron. I stuck the thin end between the jamb and the edge of the door above the lock. I levered the door back from the jamb about half an inch, raised my knee to hold the iron and yanked hard on the knob. The wood splintered, the door opened, the iron fell on the ground and I fell on my fanny.

I dusted off my pants and walked into the evil-smelling vestibule. Some of the trash had been picked up and stuffed into the cans. The kitchen door was open and I went in there and lit a match. It looked the same as before, except that Bill Denton was no longer there. I tried to find a light, but there wasn't any and I went into the bedroom where I'd found Joey and Stella and turned on the dim lamp on the dresser. The cigarette lighter, the spoon and the glass of water were gone. The bed was still mussed from them lying on it.

As I remembered, she had flung her arm toward me when I startled her with my entrance. But it had been a scrap of paper and it could have drifted to rest almost anywhere.

The lamp had a six foot cord on it. I lifted it off the dresser and looked in the nearest corner. There was nothing but dust. The cord wouldn't reach to the next corner and I got down on my knees and lit a match. More dust, a few scraps of paper, but only scraps, old and yellow and meaningless.

I pulled the bed out from the wall and looked along behind it, with the same results. Besides trash and dust there were cobwebs. I pushed them out of the way. I had begun to have a frantic feeling and I even snarled at them, then caught hold of myself and counted for a while till I got quieted down. I held still on my hands and knees, letting my head sag to relax my neck and shoulders. And pretty soon, in a slow, long-delayed reaction, I realized I had been staring for some time at what I had set out to find. I didn't even need light. I just reached out and picked it up—the torn-off back of a paper matchbook. I put it in my pocket. I had never learned how to read in the dark.

The little finger of my right hand rested on a crack in the floor. I brushed some of the dust out of the way and ran my finger along the crack. It came to a corner where the crack made a right angle turn. I lit another match and found a trapdoor three feet square, with a shiny brass ring in the middle of one side. I pulled on the ring and the door came up. I pulled it all the way up, let it fall back onto the floor and looked down into darkness. By the aid of another match I found a steep stairway leading down and, along the underside of the trapdoor, a light switch. I pressed it and light stabbed whitely at my eyes.

When I could see again I got one foot into the hole and onto the top step, lowered myself through the door and went on down. At the bottom of the steps I looked around, blinking.

A flimsy wood partition ran from somewhere in the dark rear of the building and ended abruptly fifteen feet from the steps and a little short of them. Nailed to the old, scratched framework was a wooden plaque that read: Grand Avenue Boys' Club. Beyond the partition was a larger room, brightly lighted. I went in there through the gap between the end of the partition and the edge of the near wall of the larger room.

It was a kind of clubroom, maybe twenty by thirty feet and without windows. The air was stale and there was a heavy odor of dusty cloth. One end of the room was hung with high, pleated drapes of some gray material and on a platform in front of the drapes stood a long table, also covered with cloth in thick folds. There were three high-backed chairs behind the table. Above and behind the chairs, halfway up the wall against the drapes, was a huge wooden plaque, painted in red and white—a V-shaped mark with a human eye realistically portrayed at the top of the V. Underneath in large block letters were the words:

MR. SMITH

There were thirty or forty folding chairs scattered over the floor. On the three undraped walls hung pictures of sports figures, mostly fighters. Along one wall under the pictures was a row of steel cabinets, office type furniture, with heavy knobs, some with combination locks.

I crossed the room and opened one of the cabinets. Inside were shelves and on the shelves guns—pistols, revolvers, automatics of every kind. I lifted a couple of them out. Some of them had had numbers stenciled into the steel and the numbers had been filed off. I closed the door. In the next cabinet were knives and razors piled on the shelves, a hundred or more of them. I started picking up the knives, studying them, and suddenly I thought, Mac, what the hell are you doing here?

I had one of the knives in my hand and I weighed it on my palm. It was a well-balanced, thin, sharp, deadly thing. It weighed real good. I looked into the open cabinet and I looked up at the plaque against the drapes with the big V and the words MR. SMITH.

Why not? I thought.

I lifted the knife over my right shoulder, sighted carefully and let fly.

It was a lucky shot. The knife stuck in the middle of the eye at the wide top of the V.

So, Mac, I thought, you're real sharp with the knife, real theatrical. How are you going to find out anything here? The knife that killed Bill Denton? Go ahead, pick a knife.

I looked in at them. Some had tags on them bearing names, such as "Gug," "Brat," "Lefty," and "Killer."

So. Names.

I heard a tearing sound, glanced up in time to watch the plaque with the eye pull loose from its mounting and fall, sliding down the panel of cloth to the floor, where it stopped, still upright against the drapes, with the knife I'd thrown still stuck, quivering, in the eye.

I looked up to where it had been. I saw a hole in the drapes, a twelve-inch circle, and the dark brown cone of a loudspeaker set into the white plaster wall.

I went to the wall and made a desultory search for a way to get beyond it. But the drapes were fastened to the floor. I'd have had to tear them all out to get at it, if it was there. It was not the time for it, nor even the place really.

Because this would be only the front, the trappings—how the kids would go for it!—but not the guts, the down-to-earth, fundamental guts of the organization. Those would be found in only one place—in some guy's mind. And there were no guys' minds lying around on this dusty floor.

And if you don't get some sleep, I told myself, your own mind will be lying on some dusty floor, trying to get picked up and put to bed.

I went back to the stairs, climbed up, switched off the light and lowered the door. I didn't bother to replace the bed against the wall. Let somebody else replace it. Replacing was not my business.

I thought that over as I went back through the kitchen and the smelly vestibule to the alley.

What is your business? I thought. Who knows? This is a business? This prowling through an endless night looking for shadows?

It took me quite a while to get a grip on myself. When I began looking around for transportation, there wasn't any. It was two-twenty in the a.m.

and no ride anywhere in sight. I walked along the dark street, lost now, trying to remember the direction to my own place, unable to remember, looking ahead for a busy corner where I might find a bus or car line.

I must have walked around the same two blocks a couple of times before I found anything familiar. What I found was the long row of dirty, twisted spikes in the iron fence at the end of Francie's block of tenements and the gone-out, dead sign over the cigar store. I walked along slowly, letting my fingers dance loosely across the spikes, the way I'd done as a kid, heading now for familiar territory, and somebody came into sight— somebody small and tight and running like hell. His feet thudded on the walk and he ran right into me because I didn't try to get out of the way.

He jumped back, dodged and started off. I grabbed his arm and held him tightly. He began to fight. Then I pulled him up close and he looked at me and quit fighting with a kind of contempt.

"Kind of late, isn't it, Spig?" I said.

He sneered at me.

"Leggo," he said, "for Chrissake!"

I let go of him. He stood there, eyeing me and I wanted to say something to him, but there wasn't anything. I just looked at him and breathed and then he said, "So long, jerk!" and ran off, his feet thudding, fading on the walk.

Now I knew real plain where I was and where I stood. I walked the few blocks to the corner where the streetcars ran. I leaned against a lamppost to wait and while I waited I fished in my pocket for the fragment of match-book I'd found beside the bed where Stella had thrown it. I held it up close. There were numbers scratched on it in pencil, barely legible on the slick, laminated surface of the pasteboard. The numbers were: *12-4890.* There was nothing except the numbers.

I put it in my wallet. They could be a serial number for almost anything, or a code or an auto license number. As soon as I got home, I would call the cops and let them go to work on it. I was no cryptographer.

After about twenty minutes, a car came and I climbed on and rode to my own corner. I would have enjoyed a cup of coffee, but everything was closed up tight. I walked to my building and up to my floor. I felt around in my pocket and I had no key. I tried the door, but it was locked. I looked some more for the key, without success.

I leaned against the door, thinking it over. It would be a shame to bust the door down, wake everybody up. The manager of the building lived two blocks down the street. It would be a shame to wake her up just for a key.

Also, it would be a big, fat shame for me to sleep on the cold, hard floor in the cold, dark hall of the tired old building.

So we will go and wake up the manager and get a key, I told myself. We will go right now and a pity it's such a long walk.

I went back to the stairs and started down. I got down one flight and heard heavy feet ascending from below. I stopped, waiting. There were no other sounds, only the feet climbing, clomping on the old wood of the steps. It was silly to stand there in the middle of two floors. I backed up the flight I had just come down till I stood at the top, with one hand on the newel post, and watched them come up.

There were five of them. First the District Attorney, second, Austin Clark, third, Dr. Stein. And behind them two cops—the same two cops who had come to see Joey at Francie's apartment a few hours before.

They came up in single file and the D.A. looked a little startled when he saw me waiting at the top of the steps. But if he was startled, he was certainly not amused.

What the hell now? I thought.

They crowded into the space around me in the hall and the D.A. looked grim. Likewise with Clark and Stein. The two cops just looked tired.

"Gentlemen?" I said.

The D.A. motioned back toward my apartment.

"Inside," he said.

We all went back to my door.

"I don't have a key," I said.

"Too bad," he said, nodding at the cops.

They looked at each other, drew lots mentally, and then the silent one, who was bigger than his partner took a sight on the door, rushed it and busted out the center panel. It made a hell of a noise. He reached in through the hole in the door and opened it from the inside. The D.A. motioned us inside.

It was not the way men come on a friendly visit and I couldn't guess what was up. I stepped in and switched on a light. The D.A. came in and the rest of them followed him, first Clark, then Stein, then the two cops. I looked at the D.A.

"All right," I said. "What?"

He didn't answer. He had a manila envelope in his hand and it looked like the one his secretary had brought him while I sat in his office. He looked at me as if it would have been a pleasure to strangle me where I stood. Then he ripped open the envelope, tore something out of it and threw it on the floor. I looked down. What he had torn out of it was a group of photographs, 8 x 10 enlargements. They lay in a raggedly fanlike pattern on the rug. A couple of them were face up. I looked at them.

They were pictures of Stella Perino. Stella Perino was naked. Stella Perino was on my bed. My bed was in the other room. There was no way to identify it as my bed, except that if you were to go in and take a look, you would have no trouble recognizing it—by the spread, by the wallpaper in the background, and any number of other items clearly visible in the pictures.

The D.A., Clark and Stein were ranged in a little arc across the pictures from me. The two cops leaned against the wall beside the door. Dr. Stein cleared his throat. I looked at the pictures again. Two of them were face down. I knelt on the rug and flipped them over slowly, using my fingernail only. They were more or less the same as the first two.

I climbed up to my feet. Dr. Stein cleared his throat again.

"I'm sure there is some reasonable explanation—" he rumbled.

Clark picked it up.

"Naturally there is. Mac—"

I shook my head.

"Not for this gentleman, there isn't," I said. "He's been looking for a way out from under us since midnight. Now he's found it. I don't know how, but he's found it—"

"But look—" Clark said.

The D.A. held up his hand. It was shaking.

"Go ahead," he said to me. "Tell me. I hear it every day, I might as well hear it from you. Tell me you've been framed."

"All right," I said. "I was framed."

My mouth felt like a wad of warm candle tallow.

"It's perfectly evident he was framed," Clark said. "I wouldn't know whose bed that is. Would you, Mr. District Attorney?"

"It won't take long to find out," the D.A. said.

He looked around the room, then charged into the hall that led past the bathroom to the bedroom. Clark and Stein followed him reluctantly. The cops stayed where they were. I followed the others down the hall to my bedroom. The D.A. had the door open now, had found the switch and turned on the light. Clark and Stein were peering past him into the room. I peered past all of them. I was pretty numb by now and the shock didn't hit me very hard.

She was there all right, sitting straight up in my bed, in her birthday suit, staring wide-eyed at all of us, holding the sheet coyly up in front of her. I saw her eyes travel across their faces, start to swing away, then come to rest on my face.

"Mr. Donnelly! Why didn't you tell me these men were coming?"

I turned around and walked stiffly back into the living room. I heard the bedroom door slam, the tramp of their feet, and turned to see the D.A. dragging an official-looking document out of his pocket. He held it out in his trembling hand, then tore it to pieces, slowly and methodically, letting the pieces flutter like snowflakes to the floor.

"That's our contract," he said tightly. "That's what I think of it. I'll leave the pictures too. You might want them as souvenirs. I have the negatives. For your information, we have trains for Chicago every two hours. Unless the girl decides to press it, I will spare the city—and myself—the embarrassment of an arraignment. We can always find you."

He went to the door, yanked it open and looked back at Clark and Stein. Stein was staring first at me, then at the pictures on the floor. The D.A. spoke from the door.

"I have some things to discuss with you two gentlemen," he said. "If you want to commiserate with your golden boy later, that's up to you."

Clark started out, pausing long enough to give me a slight slap on the shoulder. Dr. Stein whispered hoarsely, "I call you later."

"I may not be in," I said.

They went out. The door closed after them. I noticed that the two cops were still with me, stiff and empty-faced against the wall. I tried to grin at them with my useless mouth. It felt like nothing—nothing at all.

I found my bottle and three clean glasses and made three drinks. I took two of them to the cops, who accepted them and stood there, looking at me, or at each other or at the wall or at nothing.

CHAPTER THIRTEEN

I guess it was ten minutes we stood there in silence, drinking, looking at each other, or at the wall or at nothing. The pictures of the nude Stella lay on the floor and now and then I looked at them. Just for a change. They were lousy pictures. They had been taken in a hurry and carelessly. After all, there hadn't been much time that they could count on. Beasly and his pal Slim had tried to make time, not knowing whether I was heading home or not, and they had done pretty well. Stella had no doubt lifted my key from my coat in Francie's kitchen. Louis could have set it up while we were all in Joey's room. Anyway, there had been plenty of time.

So really, the guy with the camera, whoever he had been, could have done a much better job. He had a willing subject, well stacked and young and fresh. But of course, he couldn't have known...

When did it occur to them? I kept wondering. When did they find out? What was the hour? Or the tip? What had told them? Or who? Or was it whom? I might never know. My days as a schoolteacher were assuredly numbered.

There was a sound from the hallway and the three of us looked in that direction.

It was little Stella, pretty Stella, in her sweater and flaring skirt, bare legs and white, flat shoes, with a small purse dangling in front of her; Stella walking demurely out of the hall toward the door while we watched. She walked with short, mincing strides and when she got within reach, I put out my hand and she stopped automatically, as if she had been a wind-up toy.

She looked at me briefly, then her eyes dropped.

"Why, Stella?" I said. "Why?"

She wouldn't look at me.

"I'll go now," she said, moving away.

So I let her go and she got to the door and the cops let her go too, because after all, they were cops and they had been told what to do and they would do it till they dropped. But as she opened the door, I said:

"Be careful, Stella. You probably don't know what you've done. But the guy who set it up—he knows. He knows real well. Be very careful.

Lock all the doors and stay inside. Don't let anybody in. Be careful, Stella."

She hesitated at the door, but she didn't look back. She went outside and the broken door swung to gently behind her.

I waited for the cops to go too, but they didn't go. They stayed.

"Well," I said. "Another drink?"

They shook their heads in unison.

"Whenever you get packed," the talkative one said.

"Packed!" I said. "No kidding?"

"No kidding," he said dully.

I went to the bottle, poured myself a shot and drank it, right in front of them, slowly, savoring it, even smacking my lips.

"This is a new experience for me," I said. "I've been shown to the door a few times in my life. But I never had a personal escort out of town."

"Just get packed, huh?" he said wearily.

"What if I don't?"

They looked at each other. The talkative one looked back at me.

"Then you can leave your stuff here," he said. "But you'll go. So help me, you'll go, because we'll wait till it's done."

"I guess you would at that," I said.

He looked at me out of his bleary-eyed, scraggly face and he said, "I don't know whether I ever came up against one as tough as you or not, but I'll try it. I'll try anything."

A guy like that, you can only love him.

It didn't take long to pack. I hadn't brought much and there was only the one bag. When I carried it back to the front room, they were as I had left them, standing against the wall, waiting.

I looked at the pictures on the floor, put the bag down, opened it and threw the photos in on top, along with the pictures of the little girl in the trash can. Someday I might have the good luck to run into the guy who'd shot them. That could be quite a party.

I closed the bag again and got up stiffly. The lack of sleep and the various kicks in the face—from Francie, from Spig and Stella—had reduced me to something like a dried corn husk.

The telephone rang. I looked at it. The cops waited. It went on ringing. The talking cop said, "You want to answer it?"

I shook my head.

"Do you?" I said.

He stepped away from the wall, pulled open my battered door and held it for me. His partner went out first and waited for me in the hall. I went out there and the other cop closed the door carefully, making sure it was latched. I wanted to laugh then, but my face was too stiff.

86

We went downstairs in single file, the big cop first, then me, then the other one. They had a car outside and I got into the back seat and put my bag on the floor. The big cop got under the wheel and the other one climbed in beside me. We started off. He found a misshapen cigarette pack and offered me one. I shook my head.

We drove through the dark streets, not fast, not slow. Occasionally, we would pass another car, but mostly the place was dead. There were headlights behind us at some distance, but I paid no attention.

The last couple of miles to the depot were by way of a wide parkway with a green lawn down the middle and a lighted fountain at the junction of several interlacing drives. The depot, a rambling modern building, was on a low hill beyond the fountain and we swung up a curving drive to the cabstand, where the cop parked. I waited while the two of them got out, thinking it might as well be done properly. I climbed out after them, dragging my bag out of the car, and walked between them down a wide corridor, across the rotunda and over to one of the ticket windows. The sign over it read: COACH TICKETS—CHICAGO. I looked at the cop.

"I think I ought anyway to go first class," I said.

He shrugged.

"You're buying it," he said.

The big clock on the wall behind the ticket windows read twenty minutes to four. The next Chicago train would leave at 4:05. I bought a first class ticket and a lower berth. That would give me four hours of sleep, barring unforeseen contingencies, such as being red-lighted off the train.

When I had the ticket, the cop looked at his watch, rubbed his eyes and yawned.

"Cup of coffee?" I said.

They looked at each other and he nodded. We tramped across the rotunda, deserted except for a couple of sailors asleep on a bench, to the coffee shop.

Most of it had been closed off and the lights were dim. But there were ten stools open at the counter and behind us, near the entrance, I had seen two or three booths still open for service.

I sat down between the two cops and the girl working the counter brought coffee. I paid. I drank some of it and pretty soon I looked at the talkative cop and said, "What do you think?"

He drank some of his coffee, holding the hot cup in both hands, inhaling the steam.

"I don't think," he said. "I walk around town and ask questions and try to keep my nose clean. I'm too tired to think. I'm always too tired."

I knew how it went.

"Well, I've been thinking," I said. "I don't ask you to believe this on my account, but the girl you saw in my apartment—she was part of a frame."

"Sure," he said.

I ploughed on with it.

"That makes her pretty hot. Because there could only be one reason for framing me, as we know damn well. I doubt that the kid knew why she was doing it. But somebody knew. And if the stakes are as high as I think they are, then the girl is plainly marked. She ought to have some protection."

"Uh-huh," he said.

"The girl's name is Stella Perino. She lives on Twelfth Street—" I gave him her address. "I hope, when you get around to checking on it, you find her alive."

He didn't say anything.

"There's one more thing—besides the fact she was in on the frame they put around me, she has some guilty knowledge about the murder of the Denton kid."

He still didn't say anything, but he looked at his partner. Then he looked at his watch. We still had ten or twelve minutes to train time.

"Look," I said, "I am of Scotch descent. I have just invested about fifteen bucks in a train ticket and if I should turn it in for refund, it would cost me a service charge. So have no fear, I'll use the ticket. I'll get on the train."

They looked at each other and I couldn't tell what passed between them, but pretty soon they climbed off their stools and adjusted their hats. The big one started away. The other one looked into my face and said:

"All right. Watch your step." He turned away, then looked back. "When you get home, give my regards to Donovan. Tell him Mick Sloane said hello."

"You're Mick Sloane?"

"I worked for Donovan. Years ago. Lieutenant now, ain't he?"

"That's right."

"Well—so long, shamus."

"So long, copper," I said.

The two of them went out and disappeared somewhere beyond the rotunda. I finished my coffee and somebody was calling the 4:05 for Chicago. I pushed the cup away, picked up my change, climbed down and headed for the door where I had left my bag beside one of the vacant booths along that wall.

The booth was no longer vacant. I leaned down for the bag, started up with it, then froze in a half-crouch, looking right into her eyes.

My silver-haired mystery lady—the Duchess.

CHAPTER FOURTEEN

She smiled faintly, the way she had that first time, back in the joint where Francie worked, and I nodded and straightened up, holding my suitcase.

"Hello," I said.

"Won't you sit down?" she said.

She was the kind of woman that when she invited you to sit down, you would sit down. The caller was giving the last pitch for the 4:05 and I glanced toward the door, looked at the lady again and set the bag down.

"I'm supposed to catch that train," I said. "I'm being run out of town."

"There are frequent trains to Chicago," she said, "and you don't look like much of a runner."

"Did we have something to talk about?" I asked, still stalling, still trying to decide.

She moved her elegant shoulders in a wholly feminine kind of shrug and said, "I don't know. I've been following you around—"

"I don't know whether to feel flattered or imposed on."

"Please sit down," she said, not begging, not pleading, just offering. I had the feeling that to refuse would be like slapping her in the face.

I took one last look toward the train gate and slid into the booth. A waitress came to the table and I ordered two cups of coffee. The Duchess had an empty cup in front of her and the girl took it away.

She had green eyes and slender, clean-cut, patrician features, with a high forehead and that silver hair brushed back from it, immaculately groomed. She wore no hat. She wore a diamond and wedding band on her left hand and a heavy silver bracelet on her right wrist. No other jewelry. I couldn't guess her age. Maybe forty, but then again, maybe in her late twenties. But she had poise and she had taken awfully good care of herself. Her skin was clear and alive, without wrinkles or pouches anywhere. Then I saw that her makeup was thick and extensive and maybe she went to a lot of work to give this impression of youth and freshness.

"The gentlemen who just left me," I said, "were policemen. If they should come back and find me still here, things might be unpleasant."

"They obviously trusted you," she said. "I don't think they'll be back. But we don't have to stay here."

There was a large red handbag on the table and she reached for it and missed, just by a hair, but she missed. She recovered almost immediately, got hold of it, snapped it open and found a package of cigarettes. But I had seen what maybe was one missing piece in the puzzle. She was stoned to the eyeballs.

I found a match in my pocket and held it for her while she lighted the cigarette. She was perfectly steady, and after she had it going, she drew a long puff, settled back against the plastic-surfaced cushion and let the smoke out slowly from her nose and mouth. It was a nice mouth. It smiled at me again, but crookedly this time.

"So the lady is a lush," she said calmly.

"The lady is not alone."

"Not at the moment, fortunately. If you're curious, being a lush is pretty much a full-time job. The lady is not anything else."

The waitress brought our coffee and went away. She dug into her red bag again and came up with a small silver flask, unscrewed the top and offered me a shot, holding it over my cup. I put my hand over my cup and shook my head. She gave me that one-sided smile again.

"The gentleman is no lush," she said.

She emptied the flask into her cup. It looked like brandy. She put it away and snapped the bag shut.

"You would have given me your last shot?" I said.

"Why were they running you out of town?"

"Statutory rape," I said.

She lost her smile, but not her poise.

"But why really?" she said.

I was sagging all over and I thought longingly of the lower berth that had rolled out of the depot a few minutes earlier, while I stood there like a schoolboy, flustered by a pair of drunken green eyes.

"Would it be all right if we talked about something else?" I said. "Pretend I'm a romantic secret agent on a difficult and perilous mission—"

"That much I had already figured out," she said, "except that I don't know how romantic you are."

"I'm pretty romantic, lady. Otherwise, I would be sound asleep on that train, which I missed at considerable risk to my future comfort."

"I'm sorry," she murmured and studied the end of her cigarette.

"How did you know I was a secret agent and that my mission was difficult and perilous?"

"Because I'm a little romantic too."

I couldn't hold up my head any more. I slapped my hands against my cheeks, rested my elbows on the table and propped myself there.

"How about your mission?" she said.

"Somebody messed with the script. I got through Act I all right and was all set to finish Act II with a smash and then they ran in some new lines and—Oh, Christ, what are we talking about?"

"You're in the toils of a neurotic woman, who couldn't bear to see you go away. I owe you something. I can offer you lodging, food, drink and seclusion, and I'm afraid that's all. No great adventure, no roll in the hay, no hashish."

"It's friendly of you, ma'am," I said, "but I don't think the Cameron household would be the place for me—" If I had startled her, she gave no sign of it.

"It must have been the picture on David's desk," she said.

"All right," I said, "you're still ahead of me. If you've finished your coffee, let us get into a closed vehicle of some kind, so that I will stop feeling like a sitting duck."

I left some money on the table for the coffee and she slid out of the booth. She was perfectly steady on her feet and she walked ahead of me out of the coffee shop and across the rotunda with a clean, aristocratic stride, the handbag dangling at her side, and you would have had to look very sharply to see anything amiss about her. Which, of course, was the way it had to be for her.

There were several cabs and we got into the first one. I threw my bag into the front seat and settled down beside her in the back. She had already murmured an address to the driver and we rolled quickly down the curving drive and onto the parkway.

"Do you spend a lot of your time this way?" I said.

"Indeed! Practically all of it."

"And you only pick up romantic secret agents who are on difficult and perilous missions?"

She laughed softly.

"Oh now. I'm not that lucky. I don't ordinarily pick men up at all— never for the usual reasons. This is not because I'm a good, moral woman. I'm sure you understand—"

"No, ma'am. I don't understand at all. But I'm too tired to put up a fight. So whatever the reasons—I guess for tonight you've got me."

"That's a little unkind."

"It was unkind of you to butt into my business in the first place and keep me from getting on that train, which I had promised the copper I would do."

She said nothing more then for a long time. I rested my head against the back of the seat and closed my eyes and when the cab stopped, it startled me out of a dream, the details of which I don't remember. I brought myself out of it by shaking my head, which hurt sharply, so that I quit it and fought my way out of the cab, climbing over her knees, into the fresh air, where I was able to stand and help her out, pay the driver and get my suitcase.

The cab went away. We were standing in front of a row of old, brownstone houses with white steps going up to narrow doors. There were small lawns in front of most of them and they were all well-kept and neat. This would have been the place to live in the city in the 1890's. Now it was like the Near North Side in Chicago: old, but well-kept and probably only slightly less expensive than the modern places along the parkways and on Riverside Drive.

I followed her up the steps and into the dark vestibule of one of the houses. It had been made into five apartments, two on each of two floors and a penthouse studio on top. Naturally, she led me to the penthouse. It was a long, hard climb. She hadn't turned on any lights and all I had to go by was the faint gleam of her nylon-sheathed, impeccable and somehow untouchable legs.

At the top of the climb, she got out a key, opened a door and switched on a light inside. I followed her into the apartment.

My first impression was of being surrounded by people. I cringed mentally, thinking I'd just duck back out and run for the depot. Then I found that the people were pictures. Pictures all over the place, big ones, little ones, some in frames, some on paper or canvas tacked to the walls; portraits, landscapes with figures and others that looked like they might be people but you couldn't be sure of it—mostly lines and crazy angles. Finally I saw an easel in one corner with a canvas on it and the place began to make some sense. There was a pile of canvases in one corner that I guessed there wasn't room for on the walls.

There was little furniture and what there was didn't look like much. Some small tables with Chinese cigarette boxes on them and a bowl of flowers. There was a studio couch against one wall with a lot of highly colored pillows on it. There was a window that took up most of another wall and drapes had been drawn across it. It was arty and casual and I had seen similar apartments, but I couldn't remember ever having seen so many pictures before in so small a space.

I saw that the Duchess was waiting for me in a narrow hallway that led to the rear of the apartment.

"If you'd like to bring your suitcase in here—" I followed her down the hall, past a bath and clothes closet, into a bedroom. On our right there had been an open door leading to a kitchen, with a dining nook in one corner. It was all compact, cozy and no doubt convenient.

In the bedroom were a large bed, built low to the floor, a dressing table and mirror, a chair in front of it and a hooked rug on the floor. I set the bag down and looked at the bed and it looked awfully good. But something had jarred me when the suitcase hit the floor. I had been following her as if she had had a string in my nose. A few hours earlier I had followed my own nose into my own apartment and bumped into a clearcut set-up. Now I was contemplating the private bed in the private apartment of the private wife of a prominent civic leader as if I didn't know any better.

I picked up the bag and started backwards out of the bedroom into the little hall. She watched me go and I could have sworn she was laughing. Only not with her mouth. With the eyes, the green, bright, alcoholic eyes.

"Is it too feminine?" she said softly. "Is it an unfit lodging for a man with bruised knuckles?"

"It's fine," I said. "I just got over being romantic."

"I never used the word in the deodorant ad sense."

"I know how you used it. But my life, lady, is real and earnest, and playing around with David Cameron's wife, while it might be fun, is not its goal."

"Oh, God," she said, "try to relax. If you have to have it that way, I'll put it on a business basis."

"I guess I have to have it some other way than this. Don't misunderstand me. You are beautiful and clearly talented. But sometimes you can't help a man. A man can only help himself."

I had backed all the way into the living room, or studio, or whatever she called it, and she had come along, keeping at a distance.

"They were escorting you out of town," she said. "That means you are no longer working on the difficult and perilous mission you started with, doesn't it?"

"That is correct."

"Are you working for anybody else?"

"No, ma'am. I am totally unemployed."

"What are your rates?"

"What would you want me to do?"

"I'm not sure. We'd have to talk it over."

"It would have to be talked over before I could accept. My rates are not high."

"How much will it cost for the talk?"

"Nothing."

"Do you have the time?"

I set the bag down.

"I guess you know I have."

She turned away abruptly and went into the kitchen. When she came back she was carrying a bottle half-full of whisky, a couple of glasses and a bowl of ice cubes. She set them on one of the little tables and motioned me into a chair. I took off my hat and sat down. She put ice in the glasses and poured whisky over it. I let mine sit there. I could hardly focus as it was. If the drink could help her, then welcome to her.

"I know who you are," she said. "I've known for some time."

"I guess you are not by any means alone."

"I don't know about that, but nobody has found out from me."

I nodded.

"Excuse me if I'm impolite. But how can you be sure?"

She swished the ice around in her glass, took a sip of the whisky and looked at me frankly.

"There's a way to drink almost all the time and still maintain some reserve. It isn't easy. It takes practice and judgment."

"Uh-huh."

Inside my head, somebody was working with a hammer.

"You knew who I was all this time and you didn't tell anybody?"

"That is true."

"Not even your husband?"

"It was he who told me—without realizing it. I overheard him discussing you with Mr. MacDonald."

"The District Attorney."

"I didn't think much about it at the time. But I remembered. I have one of those odd memories—for trivia."

I tried to think about it. The only thing I could think of seemed silly, even as I said it, but it was too late to get it back.

"Are you in love with your husband?"

She took another drink.

"I don't know how that follows from anything that's been said, but I'll give you an honest answer. I do not love my husband. Of course, he doesn't love me either, so it works out all right, more or less, sometimes…"

She let it trail off.

"When I saw him, he was certainly upset over you."

"Perhaps. But he didn't look like a man who'd lost the dearest thing in life, now did he? Tell me the truth."

"All right. I don't know why I care."

She was silent for a while and I found myself nodding off. My head must have jerked so that she noticed it, because I heard her saying, "I can imagine how tired you are. I know you need sleep. I won't keep you sitting here."

She was digging around in that handbag again and finally she came up with a newspaper clipping. It had been cut carefully with neat, straight edges, and it was old and fragile. She handed it to me and her hand was trembling, but only a little. She had certainly mastered the art of drinking yourself to death.

I handled the clipping carefully. It was a four-column sheet at the top, stepped down and trailing off into a single column at the lower right. I held it under a dim lamp on the table and squinted, bringing my eyes into focus slowly and painfully.

There was a three-column picture. It was a picture of a trash can on a dirty street. The banner headline across the top of the page had been torn off, but the subhead on the column opposite the picture read:

CHILD FOUND DEAD IN TRASH CAN—POLICE HUNT UN-KNOWN DEGENERATE

I folded the clipping again and handed it back.

"I remember the case," I said.

It took her a long time to wrap the clipping in whatever she had had it wrapped in, to open her purse, tuck it away inside, close her purse and pick up her glass. I waited. She drained the last of the drink and poured another.

"She was my daughter," she said.

My elbows were on my knees and I looked for a while at the palms of my hands. I let my head drop forward and rubbed my face some with my hands and then I couldn't seem to raise it up again. I remember her touch on my shoulder. I remember getting on my feet, picking up the drink she had poured me, carrying it into the bedroom and sitting propped against a couple of pillows, drinking it. I remember taking off my own shoes and some of the rest of my clothes and her covering me with something. And after that I don't remember anything for what now seems like forever.

CHAPTER FIFTEEN

When I woke, late sunlight dribbled through closed Venetian blinds. We were well into the afternoon. There was the smell of coffee. The bedroom door was closed and I was alone in the bed. I glanced at the pillow beside me and found it untouched. So she had meant it all right, about no roll in the hay.

My headache had subsided, but I was stiff all over and I knew it would take some moving around to bring me to life. Moving around did not appeal to me. I lay on my back with my hands under my head and looked at the ceiling and wondered how she got away with it. A woman couldn't hide in an apartment like this in a city of this size from anybody who knew how to look for her.

There was something maybe in that. Maybe he only hired incompetents to look for her. Maybe he didn't want to find her, but only to prove that he'd tried. That would be possible. Only what if one of the stumblebums he hired should just happen to stumble onto her?

Then, I supposed, he could be bought off. Or maybe she just kept moving all the time.

With all those paintings and art objects? Huh-uh. This was the kind of place you tried to make into a home. I wondered how far she had succeeded. It would be hard for her to find a home. Everything would be hard for her. It had always been hard. Because the death of a daughter, even that kind of death, would not by itself automatically drive a woman to drink. Besides, that had only been six months ago. There would have been things before that, long before.

I looked at my watch, forced myself to admit that it was nearly three o'clock, forced myself to sit up and lower my feet to the floor. I found I was still wearing my socks. On the chair by the dressing table were a clean white shirt and tie, clean socks, shirt and shorts and my dressing gown. I blinked at them. My suitcase lay on its side in the corner near the door to the hall. It was closed and snapped shut.

But it had been open at some time while I slept.

Not that there was anything confidential in it—not anything to worry about. Except the pictures, including the girl in the trash can—not cleaned-up pictures like the pictures of the naked Stella and of her own dead little one in the newspaper, but plain, unretouched, clear, carefully-made pictures out of the police files. And she couldn't have missed them, because they had been on top and she would have had to dig under them to find the clean clothes.

I tried to fight off the empty feeling with a small silent tantrum. If she was going to prowl through a man's personal effects, she might expect to turn up something ugly. Whose bag was it?

And then I thought, if it were part of the job, or if she had been suddenly helpless and needed something, I would have gone through her handbag without qualms and maybe I would have found something ugly too.

You could justify anything if you worked on it long enough. And the extent to which you felt empty afterward might be due partly to how long it had been since you had had anything to eat.

I wasn't sure of the grammar, but the idea was sound.

I took off my socks, put on the dressing gown, picked up the clean shirt and shorts and opened the bedroom door quietly. The hall was clear and the bathroom door was open. I went in on tiptoe, closed the door and turned on the shower. I'd forgotten my toothbrush and razor and I went back for them. She'd laid them out, too, on the dressing table. I made it back to the bathroom all right and got under the shower. I stayed there quite a while, taking it hot and cold and lukewarm and all the ways there are. After I'd got out and rubbed myself dry, brushed my teeth, shaved and put on the clean stuff, I felt strong enough to face some things. Not too much all at once, but maybe we could work into it gradually—whatever it was going to turn out to be.

I finished dressing in the bedroom and this time when I stepped into the hall, she met me between the living room and kitchen.

"Good morning," she said. "It's a fine afternoon."

"It was a fine bed," I said, "with the sleep built in."

She was dressed in casual clothes—blouse and flaring skirt, slippers and bare legs and her hair, instead of being done up in that smooth, immaculate coiffure of the night before, hung free around her shoulders. She looked younger and more vital. But her makeup was casual too and in the light of day I could see the marks, faint but sure, around her eyes and mouth—the marks of her illness.

"Coffee?" she said.

"With pleasure."

I followed her into the kitchen and she indicated a chair beside a steel-and-plastic table in the dining nook. There was an electric percolator in the center of the table and two sets of cups and saucers.

"Eggs?" she said. "Bacon? Toast?"

"Maybe a little later," I said, inhaling the coffee with gratitude.

I inhaled quite a lot of it before I could get around to my speech which I had worked on carefully in order that it might be short and sincere.

"I'm sorry I folded up," I said. "I'm sorry I let you sit there alone with it."

"I've been sitting alone with it for a long time."

"I'm also sorry you had to find the pictures in my suitcase. But I thank you for laying out my clothes."

There was a pause then.

"The nude girl—" she said. "Was she the reason they were showing you to the train?"

"She was the reason, though not all by herself."

"There's a name for it, isn't there? The 'badger game'? Something like that."

"There is such a thing, but this wasn't handled according to the rules. This was just a quick, improvised frame." She filled our cups again.

"You didn't put up any fight over it—as an injustice?" she said.

"No. There was no room to fight in. Besides, it would have come down to fighting with a couple of cops and they were good cops, doing what they were told. Besides again, they probably would have knocked the hell out of me. I was tired."

"You must be tired a great deal of the time."

"Frequently."

She got up from the table and disappeared into the hallway. When she came back she had a sketch pad in her hand. She handed it to me. There were half a dozen sketches. I looked at them carefully.

"This is me?"

"The first three I did from life, while you sat up in bed with the drink, just before you went to sleep. The next two I did from memory, of the moment just after I showed you the clipping about—Arline. The last one is imaginary, a kind of projection."

I looked at them again.

"I looked lousy, didn't I?"

"I was full of my own pain. I didn't see yours till after I'd done these. I got to thinking about it. What I did to you wasn't fair. You might have agreed to almost anything—just to get some rest."

I looked for a long time into her face, seeing how good a face it was, wondering how long it could last under that beating from inside.

"So I'm off the hook?" I said.

She turned away.

"You're off—the hook."

Three cups of coffee on top of the shower had got me on my feet. I went to the kitchen window and looked out along the row of old houses fronting the quiet street. Some kids were playing on the grass in front of one of them.

"No," I said, "not really. I'm not off the hook. You never get off. They slam it into you the day you're born and you never really get off. Only sometimes, you can learn to make yourself more comfortable on it. Your way is one. I guess you can get to a point where you don't feel it much. Some people sleep a lot. Some people eat all the time and get fat. One way or another—"

"And how do you do it?" she said.

I thought it over, but I didn't get anywhere with it.

"I guess I'm just lucky. I get a chance now and then to blow my top. It helps."

Pretty soon she said:

"I don't think that's the whole answer. I think you're healthier than most people. God knows how you stay that way. God knows why a man would go into your kind of business."

"God knows," I said. "But I'm not off the hook. Because there's more than your little girl—though that's more than enough for you. There's Joey and Stella—and then there's Bill Denton."

She picked it up so quickly that I turned from the window to look at her.

"Bill Denton?"

"Yeah. Bill Denton is dead."

She closed her eyes. I thought she was going to fall and I stepped in to catch her. But she held on and when she opened her eyes, they were clear.

"Not Bill Denton," she said. "There's a mistake. I can't believe—"

"I'm sorry. I guess I thought you knew so much already, you'd know that too."

"I didn't know."

"Was he a special friend of yours?"

She stood there in the middle of the room, staring at me, rigid and pain-struck, and then she beckoned and I followed her into the hall and on into the studio. She found a pullcord beside the wide window and drew the curtains back. Sunlight flowed into the room, lighting the pictures on the walls. She pointed to one of them, a charcoal sketch of a little boy.

"That's Bill Denton when he was four years old," she said. She found another, a bigger one, in oil. "That's Bill Denton at twelve."

She moved, rushing, across the room, bumping into the little table on the way. She jerked open a drawer, felt through it and found a worn, white envelope, dumped the contents onto her hand and gave me a fistful of snapshots.

"Those are Bill Denton," she said, "all ages."

She had gone to the pile of canvases in the corner and was tugging them out, throwing them on the floor behind her, looking for something. She found it, a big canvas, the edges ragged on the back beyond where they had been tacked to the frame. It was a large portrait, head and shoulders, of Bill Denton. He was wearing a sports shirt, open at the neck, and there was a lot of light in the background, yellow and orange, and it was a hell of a good picture. I guess it's not the proper test, but I'd have known him all right. There was a lot in his face that I'd never seen in it, but she knew him better than I did.

I stood there holding it, studying it, and then I began to think of the last time I'd seen him, in the blood, on the dingy floor, with Stella giggling on the other side of the wall. I held it out to her, but she didn't move to take it. I laid it on the studio couch.

"Excuse me," I said, "it's a fine picture. But I saw him—not long ago. I was the one who found him. It wasn't the same."

She was rigid again, staring, as she had been in the kitchen, and finally she moved, gropingly, toward the table where the bottle from the night before still held a couple of shots. She poured it into a glass, picked it up and drank it, leaning on the table, supporting herself on one hand. She drank it all and put the glass down, tipped up the bottle and saw it was empty. She gazed at it as if it were some kind of snake or something, then whirled with it still in her hand and let go. It smashed into one of the pictures on the wall. The picture had been behind glass and that shattered and dropped in splinters along with the broken bottle. The next thing I knew, she was yelling, "I can't stand it any more! The pictures! The dreams! I cant stand it!"

She ran from the table before I could move and grabbed up the broken neck of the whisky bottle. She began to slash at the pictures, cutting across them with the jagged glass. A couple of them fell from the hooks and she kicked them out of the way and went after another. By that time I had hold of her arms and I slid my right hand carefully out toward her wrist till I could reach her hand and hold it still. She struggled to get away and I had to hold more tightly than I wanted to. Her hand twisted and the glass fell out of it and she stopped fighting as suddenly as she had begun. She leaned against me, panting, letting me hold her until the awkwardness of the position forced her to move and she pulled away and went back to the table. After a while her breath came easier. She shook her hair back out of her face, glanced at me, then looked away.

"I seem to be full of big talk," she said. "Did I say something about learning how to drink?"

"I don't remember. I don't think it was the drinking."

"Why did you stop me? They're my pictures."

"I don't know. It must be a little like trying to stab yourself. Only instead of blood, you draw paint. The oil, I understand, never really dries."

"That sounds awfully profound."

"If it's profound, then I don't know."

"Why?" she said, beating on the table with her clenched fist, talking only to herself now, "why couldn't I have met a man who knew where he stood in the world—before it was too late?"

"I'm not sure what you mean, but they tell me it's never too late."

Still watching me with the bright green eyes, she ran her hands through her silver hair. She held them out in front of her, staring at them. She ran a finger along a wrinkle in the front of her skirt.

"Excuse me," she said. "I'll try to make myself presentable."

"Likewise," I said. "I'd like to go out and get a paper."

"Of course."

I went into the bedroom and found my hat. When I came out, heading down the hall toward the front door, she was standing in the studio doorway, watching me. Her face looked haggard now, no longer fresh and vital as it had earlier.

"You'll come back?" she asked.

"I'll come back. You'll promise me something?"

"If I can."

"You won't do any more cutting up of pictures, or touch any of the glass?"

She looked at her feet. Her face was flushed.

"No," she said, "I won't."

"I'll be back."

She came across the small entryway and put a hand on my arm. Almost at once she took it away again.

"If the police pick you up—you couldn't come back, and maybe I'd never know—" I mustered up a grin.

"Old Mac never breaks a promise to a lady," I said.

She smiled back at me. It was sporting of her. It must have cost quite a lot.

"All right, Old Mac," she said. "Go get your paper."

"You can leave off the 'old' part of it. Call me Mac."

She smiled some more.

"You're doing real good," I said.

"Laugh and the world..."

I went out, hearing her close the door quietly. I got fifteen feet down the upstairs hall, the door opened again and she came out, looking at me shyly. I stopped.

"Is that all the name you've got?" she said. "Just 'Mac'?"

"You ask a mighty personal question."

"Well then. Go get your paper."

"Be sure to wash behind your ears."

She smiled again, still shyly, and went back inside. I went down the stairs. The knot had begun to form in my stomach as soon as she'd closed the door, but I was on the street and halfway past the first block of houses before it turned into a real thought.

It worked both ways, didn't it? What if I should go back and she wasn't there? What if somebody should find her and take her away while I was gone? Then it would be me who might never know.

I turned around and started back, then stopped.

You'd make a great couple, wouldn't you? I thought. She getting oiled every day and you out banging around. I could see the nightly homecoming, after the first thrill had faded, her with the bottle in front of her on the table, looking up, saying something like, "Well, which poor deadbeat did you put the arm on today?"

And me saying something like, "Ah, the hell with it," and sitting down to sort out the unpaid bills.

A great life, hull, kid, Duchess, pal, sweetheart?

I walked three blocks to a group of stores. There was a lunchroom with a newsrack in front of it and I picked out two afternoon papers and went in and ordered ham and eggs. After a little fortification from the hot coffee, I brought myself to spread out the first paper and take a look.

The D.A. had certainly broken the story. He'd broken it wide open and spilled it in big, black letters all over the front page.

HIGH SCHOOL BOY MURDERED
YOUTH GANGS ON WARPATH.

He'd got his name in the lead all right.

District Attorney MacDonald said today all available police have been called to emergency duty to deal with rat-pack terrorism in downtown area. Following discovery last night of the slashed body of a high school boy, William Denton, son of Mr. and Mrs. Clarence Denton, etc., etc.

The story didn't have much to say in the way of facts, beyond the simple ones that the boy had been found, that he had been murdered, that the method indicated a youth gang attack with a vengeance motive, and that police were rounding up suspects.

It was reported that many pupils of the West Avenue High School had been absent and there were ominous gatherings of youths, even in the normally quiet "uptown" section. A teen-agers' party had been scheduled for this evening in that neighborhood. Many of those attending would be close friends of the murdered boy. Police had decided to permit the party to be held, but said a close watch would be maintained on activities.

There was a statement by Attorney David Cameron, Chairman of the Citizens Committee on Juvenile Delinquency, urging the citizens to be calm, and there was a front page editorial in twelve-point type, wondering how it happened that the District Attorney had sat on the story for six hours before releasing it to the press. The editorial implied a conspiracy of silence, to cover for districts from which the D.A. drew heavy support in the last election, etc.

The last paragraph of the editorial read:

> It is rumored that certain city fathers had bypassed legally constituted enforcement agencies by hiring an anonymous undercover agent to work in one of the schools—a private eye from Chicago. If this is the way, etc., etc.

If they had enough to go on to print the rumor, they probably had the rest of it. Not that it mattered now.

There was a four-column picture of the alley entrance to the apartment where Bill's body had been found and an inset of Bill in baseball uniform, taken from the sports files. In a separate story it was recalled that Joey Arvin, a "downtown" kid, had been hit in the head by a pitched ball thrown by Denton and that police were waiting to question him. But he was under the care of a doctor and could not be reached at this time. So Dr. Stein was still holding his piece of the fort.

Austin Clark's name was not mentioned in any of the stories. Neither was mine. The story petered out on the second page because they didn't have enough to spread it any farther.

I leafed through it, skimming the international and national news and was about to pick up the other paper when an item in the back pages caught my eye.

DETECTIVE OFFICER HIT-AND-RUN VICTIM.

There was a small picture with the name under it:

Mick Sloane, City Detective.

The story read:

A city detective, Mick Sloane, member of the force for fourteen years, was found dead in the 800 block of Twelfth Street early this morning, apparent victim of a hit-and-run driver. Officer Sloane was on duty at the time and had been with a partner, George Morris, until a few minutes before the accident. Officer Morris stated he could not reveal the nature of their assignment, but doubted that there was any connection between it and Sloane's death. Detective Sloane is survived by his widow, Mrs. Elma Sloane, a native of this city, and one child, a boy of nine years. Police are looking for the death-dealing vehicle.

I kept reading over and over the words:

"Detective Sloane is survived by his widow, Mrs. Elma Sloane… and one child…"

I forced some more coffee down my throat, pushed the paper away, finished the coffee and went outside. I started back to the apartment, remembered something and went into a liquor store where I bought a bottle to replace the one she'd finished and broken.

The shadows were long now and the sun would disappear early because of a haze in the west. Along the residential street, mothers were calling their kids in to supper.

I kept thinking of the worn, shaggy face of Mick Sloane, the sagging way he'd walked out of the depot coffee shop, after I'd told him about Stella.

I did not think Stella had driven the car that killed him. But I would have given a hundred to one she had been in it at the time.

Where now, Stella? I thought. Where are you going?

Any answers—Mr. District Attorney?

CHAPTER SIXTEEN

She had left the door unlocked and when I went in, she was sitting on the couch and the hazy, red sunlight gleamed in her now done-up silver hair. She had dressed for the evening and she was the Duchess again, as I had first seen her, though the dress was different, the shoes, and the hair-style slightly different too, as if she could do anything she pleased with it and make it come out neat, immaculate, undisturbed.

She sat very still watching me.

"You didn't get the paper?" she said.

"I got it."

I went to the table to set down the bottle I'd brought, but it was covered with a miscellaneous assortment of papers, cards and scraps of one kind and another. They had writing on them, mostly in pencil, and the hand was loose and scrawling.

I looked at her, holding the bottle in my hand.

"You brought that for me?" she said.

"Well, I might have one with you."

She moved on the couch and I held up my hand.

"I'll get some glasses," I said.

I took the bottle to the kitchen, opened it, got some ice cubes in a bowl and carried them back to the studio. Because the table was covered, I set the drinking stuff on the floor at her feet. I put ice in the glasses, poured a shot in my own glass, handed her a glass and the bottle. Her fingers trembled some as she took them and she avoided my eyes. I took my own glass and started across the room, pausing to glance down at the table.

"They belonged to Bill Denton," she said. "They were notes and things —he left them with me. He's been leaving them with me for two years."

"What are they about?" I asked.

"I never read them," she said. "They were his and he gave them to me so they would be in a safe place." Her voice changed, lowered. "He thought it would be a safe place."

"I think it was," I said. "As safe as a place can be. There's no truly safe place."

"It would be all right, I think, if you want to look at them."

"You must have a general idea of what they're about."

"Yes."

I waited, looking at the litter on the table, but not reading any of the words, not touching any of it. I looked up once, wondering where she had put the portrait of him that I had laid on the couch. It was not in sight. The canvases she had scattered had been restacked. But she had not touched the splinters of glass along the wall nor taken down the broken, scarred paintings that remained.

"It was sometimes very hard with Bill," she was saying. "Normally, those scraps and fragments would have been poems and love letters from a young boy to an ideal woman—older, very glamorous—you know. He was sensitive and he had wonderful imagination. But I couldn't let him fall in love with me. I think he did, for a while—I probably let him in spite of myself."

She paused and I heard whisky gurgling out of the bottle.

"Bill's mother and I were close friends. I married first and it was quite clear by the time she had married and had Bill, that—David and I would never have any children. She knew how much it meant to me. She named David and me godparents and we went through the formal part of it and all—but privately, to me, she made another promise—that she would think of Bill as partly mine, that we would be co-mothers, so to speak, that if anything should happen to her—well, I guess it was all a little sentimental and dreamy—but she meant it. And she shared Bill with me. She kept her end of the bargain. My end of it we didn't speak of, but we both understood it."

She had said all this in a low monotone, reciting facts, filling me in. Now her voice changed again and I heard some of that desperation in it, such as had broken out when she slashed the pictures.

"And I kept my end too! I really did. But it was awfully hard. A boy can't have two mothers. One is more than enough. I thought he might have one mother and one friend—one woman who would be completely safe…to love, to confide in, to learn—for whatever reason a boy needs a woman. I never tied any strings to him. I let him come and go on his own terms—mostly. Sometimes I had to coax or trick him into sitting for me. But I had to do that. I had to have something I could keep, something that would never go away."

There was another pause and when she started again she had that hysterical edge under her voice and I looked at her, hoping she had set the bottle down somewhere. And she had.

"I did everything the best way I knew how—for him. I must have been good for him. But he was never mine. The girl was never mine. Nothing in my whole life—*nothing* was ever mine!—except this place and these pictures and the dreams—the horrible, sickening dreams."

"Listen—" But she wasn't finished. Her voice dropped again and she brought the words out hollow and thin, like vomiting after you've already lost everything. It must have felt much the same to her.

"So now there's a new dream, the worst one yet. Because I killed him. I let him get killed. I let him go on with it and he got killed and it's the same as if I'd done it with my own hands—" She was holding her hands out in front of her, as she had done earlier after the hysteria with the bottle and after a moment she held them toward me and looked at me direct for the first time.

"Mac—" she said, "hold them. Hold onto my hands."

I took her hands, standing in front of her, and held them. They were like ice and stiff. But she couldn't have killed anything with them—only maybe herself, if I should let go.

"What was it you let him go on with?" I said. "That stuff? The notes on the table?"

She nodded. Her hands moved in mine and I held them. I felt her stiffen, resisting, then relax again—and again she wouldn't meet my eyes.

"It was a secret project—a sort of research. He was such an idealist. He thought he could help other kids—like that friend of his from what we called the 'wrong side of the tracks'—Joey something—"

"Joey Arvin."

"Bill brought him here once. He was a beautiful boy. But he wasn't comfortable here. He couldn't wait to get out. Then that girl—I think it's the same girl you have the pictures of—"

"Stella? Bill brought her here?"

"He went with her for a while. I—had nothing against her, except that she seemed wrong for him somehow, less honest. I never said anything to him against her. But it turned out later she was Joey's girl. They had a little trouble over it."

"When was this?"

"I don't remember—a year ago maybe."

She stopped and went somewhere with her memories. I stayed where I was, holding her cold hands, and pretty soon I prodded her gently.

"About the research project—" I said.

She glanced at the table.

"I think it would be all right for you to read them."

"Shall I let go now?"

"Please. And thanks."

I let go of her hands and she folded them into her lap and for a few seconds she looked like an old, old lady. I turned to the table and began reading the scraps of writing on the cards and notebook pages. I didn't concentrate much at first because she went on talking in short spurts of sound and I wanted to hear it at the same time.

"It was only that he got in so deep," she said. "He did these things that were really dangerous, like a child playing with matches."

I held a note in my hand that read:

> *Joey won't listen. The man selling reefers at the candy store by the school is an organizer from Chicago. He only wants Joey for a pusher—so he can organize Joey's gang. Joey says he wants to keep the gang clean...*

"Some of them," she was saying, "were little more than gangsters. He'd follow them, he'd go places that I don't see how he could get into at his age. He would never tell me he was going—he'd tell me afterward. I tried to talk to him—"

> *The Blue Grotto is owned by a big syndicate in Chicago. Mr. Cameron looked it up for me. Out there they bring in a lot of stolen cars. I saw them in the back, changing plates and stripping—some of Joey's gang were helping.*

"But I couldn't forbid him to go anywhere. I asked him to talk it over with his father, but he said his father would only worry and probably make him stay home nights. He was so serious about it!"

> *Three guys from my own neighborhood stole two cars and took them out to the Grotto. I don't know how they knew about it. I wasn't there. I heard about it. Some of Joey's gang was there too. They said the other kids were trying to muscle in. There was a fight but a couple of men broke it up. One kid got his jaw broken. Nothing happened about the stolen cars. I guess it got hushed up... Joey said his club has got a Mr. Smith seal now. I don't know what he meant, but he was real happy.*

"...once I talked to my husband about it—but I had to be vague—I couldn't betray Bill's confidence—and he laughed it off. He was fond of Bill too, in his way."

> *I think I've got a line on this Mr. Smith deal. I heard two of Joey's gang talking and one said don't worry Mr. Smith will fix it... I asked Joey if I could get into his gang but he said no. Ever since the thing about Stella he doesn't trust me. But I never did it with Stella. I guess he thinks I did. I never did it with anybody. I thought of it though.*

"I should have done something about it! I should have thought of something! I could have made him give it up, if I'd used enough pressure. But I was afraid. Afraid to lose him—and he was never mine to lose."

I glanced at her, but she was under control. I picked up another note.

We got a new baseball coach this season. Mr. Hennessy is taking a leave of absence. I kind of like the new coach. He's trying to get Joey out for the team. I think he will. He seems like a guy that makes up his mind and gets it done. He could do a lot for Joey.

I left the table and poured myself a drink. It was hard to see for a minute. I felt her watching me.

"What is it?" she said. "What did you find?"

I nodded toward the table.

"Just—" I cleared my throat, "one of the notes."

"May I see it?"

I found it and handed it to her. She read it. Then she folded it carefully into a small square, put it in my hand and folded my fingers around it.

"Has anyone ever died and left you a million dollars?" she said.

"It wouldn't be the same—"

"It would be nothing. Believe me, Mac. Nothing."

I opened my hand and looked at the square of paper.

"I better leave it here for a while," I said.

"I'll put it in your suitcase."

She took it away with her and I turned back to the table and picked up another note. It had been written hastily, as if in a classroom when he should have been working on geometry or something.

I got to make Joey wake up. He doesn't know what's going on. He thinks he's running the gang—but they do this stuff behind his back. They just use him for the front and when they have to, they can make him take the rap for anything that might happen. It's all organized from outside. The older ones, like his brother Louis, do most of it and they use Joey to keep the younger ones in line. He'll be in real trouble and it'll be too late.

I found another.

I tried to talk to Joey in the hall, but he wouldn't stop. Then I had to go and hit him in the head—I don't know what happened to that pitch. The coach was swell about it.

Underneath that he had written, evidently at a different time:

I guess I better not go up to the studio anymore. If anything happens, she could get in trouble.

110

There was a sound and I looked around to see her standing in the studio doorway. I had found still another note, half-hidden under the pile I'd already been through, and I picked it up.

I know who Mr. Smith is—but I cant do anything about it. What could I do?

I dropped it to the table and picked up my hat.

"Will you let me take you somewhere?" I said. "Where there are people, lights, something going on? Someplace—"

"A safe place?" she said.

"Yeah."

"That would be wherever you are, Mac."

This was so ridiculous that I decided to let her think it over till she realized it for herself. I went past her into the hall and down to the bedroom. I opened the suitcase, dug to the bottom of it and found my gun and harness. I took off my coat, threw it on the bed and put on the gun. I was adjusting the thing when I noticed her standing in the bedroom doorway, watching me. She had put on a coat and was carrying her handbag.

"Where are you going?" she said.

"I'm going hunting."

I put my coat on.

"And the gun?"

"I might be lucky. After I catch up with him—he might try to escape."

She closed her eyes.

"Still want to go?" I said.

"You have to let me go. You have to let me help. You're an honest man. You know why I have to."

"Will you do whatever I ask you to do, even if it seems silly."

"Anything except leave you."

It was just possible that she might be able to help in certain departments.

I pawed through the suitcase again, got out one of the pictures of the little girl in the trash can, folded it twice and put it in my pocket. She watched me with her green eyes.

We left the apartment and went down to the street. It was dark now and we walked a couple of blocks and found a taxi.

CHAPTER SEVENTEEN

I gave the driver some directions and settled back in the seat. She sat beside me with her knees crossed, the handbag in her lap, and after a few blocks, she said: "What I started to say last night, about putting this on a business basis, still goes."

I didn't answer. I was busy in the head.

"Last night," she said, "I was only—I don't know how to say it—it never occurred to me to hire a private investigator to look into Arline's death. Not even last night. It was only that—I couldn't bear to have you go away—"

"Well," I said, "I'm still here."

"I knew more about you than I told you. Bill Denton told me about you —as a coach. I don't know exactly why I started following you. I was upset about Bill. It was as if something had been growing in me that was nothing at first, but turned into something as it grew. I sat there in the studio yesterday evening and I got to thinking about you and finally, I called a friend at the school and she looked up your address for me. I went to your apartment in a taxi. But you were just leaving. So I had the driver follow you. He was very good."

He had been pretty good at that. I had moved around. There was some silence.

"What I said, about putting it on a business basis—I have money—"

"Look at it this way. They've already paid me for that job. If things work out, they'll pay me some more. It's not up to you."

She said nothing.

"There's one thing—" I said. "I need some cash. I can write you a check—"

"How much?" she said, opening her bag.

"I can write a check for as much as eight hundred dollars."

She fished around and brought out a fistful of currency. I got my checkbook onto my knee and wrote a check to cash for eight hundred. She counted it out and handed it to me.

"You always carry that much?" I said.

There was a pause.

"Only recently," she said then. "I used to keep quite a lot in a small safe, in the apartment—the studio. But somebody got in there one night—I don't know who or why. Nothing was stolen. I never followed it up."

After a while I asked, "When did you last see Bill Denton?"

"A couple of nights ago. He came in for a few minutes. It was late in the evening. He was very upset—something about an accident on the ball-field. It had to do with Joey Arvin."

"I see."

"He told me then he wouldn't be able to see me for a while. I worried about him; he was so agitated, as if he had to tell me something, but couldn't quite make himself do it. I didn't dare press him. I told him he was to do whatever he thought best."

"And that's all he told you?"

"That's all. I remember it quite clearly. I felt horrible after he left. I even called his home and asked for him, without saying who I was. His father answered and said Bill wasn't home yet."

"He didn't say anything, then, about why he was upset—except for the thing about the accident?"

"Nothing."

I pulled the papers from my pocket on which the D.A.'s secretary had typed the statement from Bill's father. There were four double-spaced pages. I turned on the rear overhead light and read them.

Bill had got into the house about a quarter of six and gone upstairs to his own room where he stayed until called to dinner at six-thirty. They had ham for dinner. It was his favorite dish and he ate quite a lot. After dinner, he helped his mother with the dishes. His mother had a club meeting that night and left the house about seven-thirty. Bill's father went into his den to do some paper work he'd brought home with him, and he heard Bill's phonograph upstairs. He remembered hearing it as late as eight o'clock.

The next thing he remembered was a knock on the front door. He had started up from his work to answer it when he heard Bill coming down the stairs and he let him get it. He was deep in his work again when there was a knock on the door of his den. It was Bill and he opened the door, stuck his head in and told his father he was going out with some of the kids for a while. His father said something about the game coming up and maybe he shouldn't be out too late and Bill said O.K. and closed the door. His father noticed that he was nearly out of cigarettes and he got up to call Bill to ask him to bring him some when he came home. But by the time he got to the door, Bill was climbing into a car that was already moving away from the curb. He didn't recognize the car. He saw that one of the occupants was a girl, but he couldn't see her clearly. He gave up trying to call

Bill then and went back to work. At about nine o'clock he finished and went out to get his cigarettes, walking the three blocks to the drugstore. When he left there, he thought about his wife's meeting, which was at the home of friends in the neighborhood, though several blocks away, and he walked over there to wait for her, taking his time.

It was nine-forty-five when the meeting broke up and he and his wife started to walk home. On the way they passed a small restaurant that was still open and went in for a late snack. They left the restaurant around eleven o'clock and walked home. They were at home by eleven-twenty and, assuming Bill had already come in and gone to bed, they got ready for bed themselves. It was Mrs. Denton's custom to look in on Bill after he'd gone to bed, but this night she decided not to take the chance of disturbing him.

They had got in bed and turned out the light when the telephone rang and Mr. Denton got up and went downstairs to his den to answer it. He was disgruntled at being got out of bed and noticed the time especially. It was twenty minutes to twelve midnight. The phone call was from the District Attorney.

I folded the papers and put them back into my pocket. She was watching me.

"Just a statement—from Bill's father," I said. "Nothing new in it."

I looked out at the now familiar street, watching the buildings as we passed, and after a minute I leaned forward and tapped the driver's shoulder, asking him to pull over and wait. He parked at the curb a few feet beyond the cigar store on Francie's corner.

There were half a dozen kids hanging around the store, kids about Joey's age, a couple older. I didn't see Louis Arvin. Farther down, along the fence that enclosed the vacant lot, a crowd of younger ones were playing, boys and girls—six to nine years. We sat there and I watched them. After a while her eyes were questioning me.

"I've got a young acquaintance somewhere in the neighborhood," I said. "He may come along. If not, we'll have to try something else."

She sat, quiet and patient, waiting. I didn't know whether she'd brought her flask or not, but assumed that if she had, she would get it out when she needed it.

I couldn't find him among the kids who were playing along the fence and I was about to give it up, had leaned forward to instruct the driver, when he came in sight, diagonally across the street, approaching the group with a swagger, his feet bare, his cap at a rakish angle on his ragged head.

"You said you wanted to help?" I asked.

"You know I did."

114

"That kid—with the cap—the one that just gave the little girl a push—his name is Spig. Will you take this couple of bucks and ask him to come back to the cab?"

"Of course—"

"If he sees me coming, he'll either run or set the gang on me. To him, I'm just a jerk. I think he'll come for you. Better hold the money out where he can see it."

"What will I say?"

"Just tell him you're looking for somebody and you'd heard he was a big man around here. When you get him back here, I'll take over."

She opened the door and stepped out, holding the two bills in one hand. I watched her approach them, like a queen entering her court. I saw them spot her and the game come to a stop as they stood, waiting. She went quite close to them and I saw Spig step up and listen to her. Pretty soon she turned and he came along with her back toward the cab. The kids left behind at the fence stared after them and one of them yelled something and they all laughed. She quickened her steps and I could guess at what he had yelled.

The back door of the cab stood open and she brought Spig up to it. He started to climb in, looked up, saw me and backed out again quickly.

"What the hell!" he said.

"Take it easy, Spig," I said.

"Listen, lady—" he looked up at her.

"Please," she said, holding the two dollars out in her hand.

He looked at them doubtfully and then back at me.

"I'm hot, Spig," I said. "The cops are after me."

He gave me that deadpan.

"Yes?"

"Yeh. And I need a little information."

"How could they be after you?" he said. "You're one of 'em."

"No, I'm not. They tried to run me out of town. Didn't you hear about that?"

"No, I di'nt."

"It's true," I said. "Look, Spig. I've got to get a message to Stella Perino. Will you take it for me?"

"Stella—?"

He had been ready to say more, but something had clicked inside him and stopped the words.

"You know her, Spig?"

He hesitated.

"Yeh. I know her."

"Will you take her a message for me?"

115

He looked again at the money, at the Duchess, then at me.

"O.K.," he said.

She started to hand him the two bills and I said, "Hold it!"

She jerked them back again. Spig had been about to grab them and now he frowned and stepped back.

"What's go'n on?" he said.

"I'll write the message on a piece of paper," I said. "You take it to Stella and ask her to sign her name at the bottom. Then you tear off the bottom part and bring it back to me. Then I'll give you the money."

"Gimme the money first."

"No, Spig. After."

I pulled some paper out of my pocket, found a pencil and began to write. He held out for some time and then, with his head down, kicking at the underside of the cab, he said, "I can't take it to her."

I looked at him.

"She ain't home," he said.

"Well, do you know where she is?"

Again he hesitated.

"Nah. I don't know."

"Do you know anybody who does know?"

He shook his head, eyeing the two bills in her hand.

"I don' know," he said.

"Maybe Joey," I said.

"Joey don' know either. Joey's sore—" He shut up again, as if he'd checked himself.

"You mean Stella's just disappeared?"

He shrugged and spat into the street.

"I don' know."

I put the paper and pencil back in my pocket and leaned back in the seat.

"All right," I said. "Let's go, Duchess."

She looked startled for a moment, then moved past him, still holding the money, and got into the cab. I reached across her to close the door. Spig watched me with bright eyes. I had the door nearly shut when he grabbed the handle, jerked it open and leaned in.

He looked around carefully, especially at the driver, then spoke in a low voice, quickly.

"I think maybe Louis Arvin would know. I could take it to him."

"Why would he know?" I said, "if you don't and Joey doesn't?"

He glanced around some more and leaned in closer.

"I seen him come out of her house today—. He had a suitcase with him. Stella's old lady was yellin' somethin' at him. But Louis didn't care.

He don't care about nothin'.'"

"Did you see where he went with the suitcase?"

"No. He got in a car."

"When was this, Spig?"

"I don' know—today—after I come home from school." I pretended to think it over. Finally I settled back again.

"All right, Spig," I said. "Thanks."

He looked at me wildly.

"Ain't I gonna take Louis a message?"

"No," I said. "Louis can't read."

"He can so! I seen him—" I let him wait. His pinched, white face was frantic.

"Listen—" he said, "Joey thinks they kidnapped her—"

"Who kidnapped her?"

"That other gang—from uptown—on account of that Denton guy. All the kids think that. To get even, see? They snatched her."

I kept quiet.

"But I think Louis Arvin knows."

The Duchess was leaning forward on the seat, staring at him.

"Give him the money," I said and she handed it over.

Spig grabbed the bills and backed away.

"So long, Spig," I said and slammed the door.

I gave the driver a direction and we pulled away. We rode about three blocks and pulled up again at an intersection. I climbed out of the cab.

"Around the block for fifteen minutes," I said. "I'll pick you up on this corner."

She nodded. I started down the street. Half a block away was a neon sign over a car lot, strung with colored light bulbs.

BEASLY—the sign read. FINE USED CARS.

117

CHAPTER EIGHTEEN

It wasn't a big lot. There was a row of late-model cars that looked pretty good and behind them a couple of rows of junk that he hadn't even bothered to shine up.

There was a small office building in the near front corner of the lot and a guy inside it at a desk, reading a movie magazine. Bordering the office was a wide driveway that led into a garage. The sign over the big double door read: BEASLY—PARTS AND SERVICE. On a smaller white card beside the door were the crudely lettered words: U-DRIVE—CARS FOR RENT.

I stood at the corner of the lot and the guy from the office stepped out, yawning, and ambled up to me. He had a pinched, sick-looking face with brown patches here and there. The backs of his hands were scaly and he kept rubbing the back of one with the fingers of the other, as if it itched. He was slightly cross-eyed.

"Something in a car?" he said. "Transportation or a heavy job?"

"Something to rent," I said. "Something that will run."

He looked me over doubtfully.

"Ah—deposit is five hundred," he said, "rates run about—"

"All right. Which one can I have?"

He lost interest in me. I gathered he only collected on sales.

"The rentals are inside," he said, jerking his thumb at the garage.

He went back into the office, picked up his magazine and got lost in it. I went around the office and up the driveway to the garage. The double doors were closed but from inside I could hear clicks and hammerings. I went in through a small door at one side.

There were half a dozen cars on the floor in various stages of disassembly and a couple of mechanics. One of them was so deep in a motor that all I could see of him was the seat of his pants. The other was at a bench, pawing through tools. Neither paid any attention to me.

At the rear of the service department, in the wall on my right, was another set of big doors. They were closed but there was a small door with a clear glass panel beside them and I went on in. A row of fairly good-looking late models stood facing into the rear wall on my left. There was space behind them to back out and swing toward the service department and out to the street.

I looked around the place and nobody was in sight. There was a waist-high counter along one wall but nobody behind it. A closed office at the end of the counter had a light burning inside, but I couldn't see anyone in it. It looked as if the fat man ran a real brisk business.

I started along the row of cars, looking in at them. The third in line was a black Buick with all the gadgets, sleek with chromium trim and a little dusty. I took out my wallet, found Stella's matchbook cover and compared the number on it with the license number of the Buick. They checked, digit for digit.

I opened the door on the wheel side and looked in at the front seat, then across the back. A couple of blankets had been tossed onto the back seat, and there were newspapers on the floor. The newspapers showed dark brown stains over the black print. I dug around in the blankets and found a piece of white cloth, pulled it out. It was a woman's white nylon blouse. It too showed dark stains. There were pearl buttons on it. One of them had been torn off. I threw the blouse back onto the seat, turned to the front and pushed a button on the dash. The hood went up slowly, creaking a little. I looked in at the motor. It was a factory-rebuilt job, about two years older than the car model. Still, it was a Buick motor and would probably run.

I pushed the hood down till it snapped shut and when I turned around, there was a guy standing in the middle of the floor, watching me. I dusted my hands together as I walked out to meet him.

He was just as bored looking as the used-car salesman out front, but healthier. He reminded me of Louis Arvin and I couldn't figure that out right away, but then I got him placed. He had been one of the two zoot suits at the cigar store when Arvin had pushed me around. He was dressed like Arvin, in a misplaced attempt to be dapper in clothes that were too tight and too cheap. He looked at me without hostility but also without friendliness.

"Looking for a car?" he said, without tone, flatly, like the sound of a gloved hand slapping a brick wall.

"Yeah," I said. "I like this Buick."

"That one's not for rent. Needs some work."

"Does it run?"

"It needs some work."

"I'm used to a Buick. I like that one."

"It's not for rent."

"All right. I'll take it. How much?"

"I said—" I had my wallet out and was pulling bills out of it as if I had a million of them. I was glad to see they were mostly twenties. He watched me. A punk like him always needs money. Always.

I held out five twenties where he could see them. I hadn't checked the motors of all the cars, but the chances were good that they were all hot, that all the motors had been switched and he knew a cop wouldn't be handing him a bill for the privilege of inspecting a hot car. A cop would just get in and drive it away—or stick a seal on it and come back later.

"Guy said five hundred deposit," I said. "Here's a bill for you and if I've got half a grand besides, we ought to be able to deal. I've got it."

He stood very still for a moment, looking at the money, then he jerked his head back toward the counter and I followed him over there. He reached across the counter, pulled a pad of forms up in front of him and got a pencil out of his pocket. He wrote down the license number of the Buick and another number which must have been a code for the business.

"Identification?" he said.

I found the ID card and put it down in front of him. He glanced at it, wrote down the serial number and the name, Donnelly, and I picked it up again. He tore a strip off the bottom of the form and shoved it at me.

"Receipt," he said. "Rates are ten cents a mile. Twenty-five buck minimum. Don't drive it out of the state."

I laid down the five twenties, counted out five hundred bucks more and laid it down separately. He didn't touch any of it.

"When you back out, I'll check the mileage."

I walked across the floor, climbed into the car and turned on the ignition. When I pushed the starter button, nothing happened.

So far, so good. We were on schedule. I climbed out and started back. The money I had laid on the counter had disappeared. The guy stood there with the pad of forms in one hand and his pencil in the other.

"Won't start," I said.

"Try one of the others."

"Call a mechanic."

He stiffened a little against the counter. I was learning quite a lot. He didn't know much yet. He was still trying to play me for a schoolteacher. If I was going to be stubborn, he would have to think of something else.

"They're busy," he said. "Better try one of the others—"

"I like this one."

I went to the big doors and found a button on the wall. I pushed it and the doors ground open slowly and noisily. The one mechanic was still buried in the motor. The other had started across the floor with a couple of tools in his hand. He glanced at me.

"Come here a minute," I said.

He shifted his direction and came in. I saw that the punk at the counter had laid down the forms and was moving toward the center of the floor. The mechanic looked at him, then at me.

"That car over there," I said. "Make it run."

He peered at them.

"Which one?"

"The Buick," I said. "The big one."

He glanced at the punk again, who had stopped between me and the car.

"That one?" the mechanic said. "Hell, that won't run. Needs a lot of work, rods, everything. Somebody drove the hell out of it—"

"No it doesn't," I said. "All it needs is to have that loose cable stuck back on the battery. I could do it myself, only I don't want to get my hands dirty. I'm going to a musicale this evening."

The mechanic began to look frustrated.

"I paid for it," I said, "and I want it. Here's the receipt." He looked at the receipt, shrugged and headed for the car. The punk said:

"Hold it. I told you that car wasn't for rent. Take one of the others."

"You rented it to me," I said. To the mechanic I said, "You saw the license number. Let's get it rolling. Or shall I call the Better Business Bureau? Right now. Right from here."

The mechanic went to the car. The hood went up and the mechanic disappeared behind it. I hoped he wouldn't be too long. I thought I had the picture in pretty good focus at the moment, but it could change if somebody else should walk in, even an innocent bystander. And there was "Baby," who would be waiting at the corner.

He didn't take long. I saw the hood go down and the mechanic opened the door and tried the starter. It worked right away. He walked past me, back toward the service department.

"Thanks very much," I said.

He shrugged. I looked at the punk again.

"Back it out for me," I said.

He just stood there. I started toward him.

"Back it out," I said again, "and check the mileage." He blustered a little.

"Back it out yourself," he said.

When I got to within four feet of him, he gave in.

"O.K.," he said. "O.K."

"Back it out easy," I said, "and don't try to crack it up. Or I'll get Beasly down here and show him the deal."

He got in the car and backed it onto the floor till it faced the service department. He sat stiffly behind the wheel. I opened the door and stepped back, holding it.

"You got the mileage?" I said.

"I got it."

"Then I'll take it. Get out."

He turned slowly in the seat, pulled his legs up and planted them on the edge of the doorsill. He got his right arm up and over the wheel and then he came out, flying, right at me. Still on schedule. I twisted out of the way and caught him with a fist in the belly as he flew. It turned him in the air and he flopped on his left side on the concrete floor. He scrambled out of the way quickly, reaching inside his coat and I kicked his hand, turning him again.

"Another shiv artist?" I said. "Go look up Louis Arvin. Take some lessons."

It didn't feel very good. It was a little like fighting with a baby. He lay there on the floor, glaring up at me and he didn't know what to do. They never do.

"Get up and go in the office," I said. "All the way in."

I waited while he got up, slowly, his eyes on my hands, and backed away into the clear. I went along with him, through an open door at one end of the long counter and along behind it into the small office.

It was a bare, shabby place, made of portable partitions and there were two telephones on a scratched wooden desk. Against the wall near the desk was a four-drawer filing cabinet. A loop of electric cord hung out the top of the lowest drawer.

I motioned him into a corner.

"What's going on—?" he said.

I gave him a nasty look and lifted my hand. He backed into the corner. I hated it. They scare so easy.

I pulled open the filing drawer. Inside was a small amplifier and on top of it, a microphone on a long cord. I thought of the loudspeaker behind the "Mr. Smith" seal in the clubroom. They would need a booster some-where at that end, but it could be done. It was simple enough.

The punk in the corner tried again.

"Look—" he said.

I kicked the drawer shut and snarled at him.

"Shut up!"

He shut up. I backed out of the office, watching him.

"Don't come out till I'm gone," I said.

I pushed the office door shut and backed along the counter and out onto the floor. Out there I could no longer see him. He would know this.

I got into the car and drove out slowly into the service department. I barked at the mechanic and he opened the big front doors for me.

Traffic was light on the street, but I took it slowly down the drive and waited for a couple of cars to pass, even though I might have bulled my way out. I glanced at my watch and it was twelve and a half minutes since I'd left her in the cab. I let the motor idle down, heard it sputter, gunned it and it stalled. I set the brake, sat there for a while, then started it again. I waited for another car to pass and drifted slowly into the street, turning right toward the corner I had left—I checked my watch-fourteen minutes before.

As I straightened into the street and glanced at the rear view mirror, I saw what I'd been stalling around for. Two guys running across the street toward the garage. They were going fast and the street was dark, so I didn't recognize them. But that didn't matter. I drove on slowly toward the corner. I saw the cab draw up and I saw her step out of it onto the walk. I nosed in behind it, coming to a stop just as he pulled away again. I twisted the handle of the door and let it swing open. She glanced in from a distance, then came quickly across the walk and slid in beside me.

I looked into the mirror again and saw headlights nosing out of the garage into the street, turning in behind us.

"Good girl," I said. "Do you know where the Blue Grotto is?"

She seemed stuck for a moment and stared at me with half-open lips. Then she said:

"I've heard of it—rather notorious. A roadhouse."

"Do you know where it is?"

"It's out by the Lake."

"Do you know how to get to the Lake?"

"Yes."

"That's where we're going."

"It's about twenty miles."

"Here we go."

I had had time to study the grille of the car behind, that had come out of the garage and was drifting slowly along the curb toward the corner, where the light was changing to green. The grille was highly polished and the gadget on top at the front of the hood was an added accessory, very fancy, like the figurehead of a ship. It looked like a nude dancing girl standing on one foot with her arms out. It would be easy to keep in sight.

At the light change I pulled ahead, straight across the street.

"You might use the parkway past the station," she said, "to get to the edge of town. That's three blocks ahead and a right turn."

I nodded. I was driving slowly along the street and the car with the figurehead came right along, staying well back. She noticed my preoccupation with the mirror.

"Are we being followed?" she said.

"I hope so."

Then I realized that didn't make any sense.

"I'll try to explain it later. Would it be too rough to tell me something about the little girl?"

There was a long wait.

"It would be rough," she said. "I'll try, Mac, if it will help."

"I can't be sure. It might help."

I made the right turn she had indicated and got onto the parkway.

"I don't want you to do it if it's too hard," I said. "Maybe it wouldn't help. Maybe I'm guessing in circles."

I studied the mirror some more and the nude dancing girl came in sight. The traffic was quite heavy on the parkway and there were four lanes on our side of it. I kept to the slow right lane and when I saw the shadow car falling into line, I began to relax about it, sure now that it would stay with us.

Beside me, she spoke in a small voice.

"Would you think it horrible of me to take a drink?"

I felt something I had felt only rarely in my life, a kind of sudden warmth for her. I had felt something like it that time Francie had touched my hand, after we'd brought Joey back from the party. It was a feeling that words alone wouldn't quite do the job. I took my right hand off the wheel and reached for one of her hands. Her hand wasn't there. Mine landed on her thigh, covered now by a topcoat, her dress and whatever underneath constituted the rest of her feminine rigging. I put no pressure on it, but I left it there for a while, trying to think up some words.

And I felt her stiffen and withdraw and when I looked at her, her head had turned sharply away, she was looking out the window. Her hands clutched stiffly at the handbag in her lap and her body was rigid with that hysterical rigidity I'd seen in her before. I got my hand back on the wheel.

"I don't think you should even ask me a question like that," I said.

The freeway was moderately filled with traffic now and I speeded up some to keep pace with the cars in the lanes to my left. I glanced into the mirror and the figurehead was still with us. I slowed suddenly and it slowed with me. I drifted, speeded up again and it came along, making no attempt to pass.

Suddenly her head was against my shoulder and her fingers twisted at my arm.

"I'm so sorry, Mac, I'm so awfully sorry and I can't explain it. I'm— Mac, can you hear me?"

"I can hear you. Let's try to relax. You better have a drink."

"You don't understand—"

"I'll have one with you. Break it out, Baby."

"Mac—" But she let go of my arm and stirred beside me. I heard the bag snap open. A few seconds later the cold hard surface of the silver flask was against my right wrist and I took it and swallowed a small shot. It was whisky and it felt pretty good. I handed it back to her.

"If I ever make a pass at you," I said, "it will be a definite, well-timed, clearcut pass and it will be unmistakable."

"Yes, Mac—"

"But now I am working, at my kind of work, and I have found that hardly ever does it happen that a pass made while working can possibly turn out to be anything better than what in the books they call a fiasco. I'm not sure what a fiasco is, but I'm sure it's something I don't have time for and I will say one more thing, which is that in the course of my work, I have been invited into some of the damnedest beds you could imagine and if I had accepted all the invitations, I would have given up this kind of work long ago because I would have gone quickly broke and no doubt would have had my head busted open time and time again. And that is all the speech I have time to make."

We were approaching the end of the parkway and there were several overhead signs. I slowed.

"You want the Ridge Route," she said.

The last sign had a big arrow pointing to the right and above the arrow were the words: RIDGE ROUTE—*Lake Thomas.* All the cars in the line ahead had turned off earlier and I could see none behind us now except the ever-faithful dancing girl, perched on top of the brightly polished grille. I gathered it was early for the Lake season.

The turn-out was a generous three lanes of concrete for a quarter-mile, then narrowed to a two-lane macadam with gravel shoulders. There were woods on both sides and after passing a few scattered homes, set well back among the trees, the road began to climb and wind through nothing but countryside. A white marker on the shoulder read: Lake Thomas *19* Miles. A speed limit sign read *45* miles, but I held it down to thirty-five, because the road was unfamiliar and I would have to pick my spot quickly, without knowing in advance just where it lay.

Except for the brief direction back on the parkway, the Duchess had been silent. She was no longer holding my arm. She had put the flask away and sat now with her hands in her lap, looking straight ahead. When she began, without warning, to talk, it startled me enough to change the pressure of my foot on the accelerator.

"David was twenty years older than I," she said. "A self-made man—the American Dream with all the trimmings. From nothing—absolutely nothing—to leading citizen; from the slums to Riverside Drive in twenty clawing, biting, fighting years. It's been done before and it will be done again and I guess some men will always have to try.

"But the price is high—out of proportion. Sometimes you lose so much, you can't ever win enough to make up for it. David had lost too much. But I was twenty-three just back from the Art Institute, and I didn't know anything about that. He was successful and rich and charming and he reminded me of my father, who had also been a successful man but hadn't had to scratch so hard for it."

The headlights behind us had drawn closer and I pushed the Buick up to forty. The road was still climbing and winding, but the curves were long and easy. The groves and woodplots on both sides grew close and I had not yet seen any side roads in any direction. The trailing car stepped up to stay with us.

She was going ahead with her story, the words low and forced, in the dark of the front seat.

"I found out very soon how much he had lost. For a long time I hung onto the romantic idea that I could help him, put it back for him.

"But you can't. Not when it's all going one way—everything going out and nothing coming back. After a while you run out. You have to get some of the love back. Even if it's only the face of love, even the ragged fringe. If that's all you can get, you settle for that.

"And I settled—for the ragged fringe—for a week of nights—in that studio—with an ardent, talented stripling, as they used to say—whom—I—had—hired to model—for me."

I didn't look at her. I could feel her moving beside me and I heard the click of her purse, the faint rasp of the cap being unscrewed from the flask.

"It hurts too much," I said. "Don't go on with it."

She had put the flask away and she said:

"No. It's strange, but it doesn't hurt the way I thought it would."

We had stopped climbing and the road had leveled off, though there were still curves, and since we had come up, surely we would go down eventually, because in this part of the country, the land is mostly flat and you would not be likely to find a lake at any height.

"Will there be a side road anywhere between here and the Lake?" I asked.

"A few miles ahead," she said, "there's an intersection. I think there's a boulevard stop."

A pair of headlights came up fast on my left and I moved toward the shoulder and slowed, ducking mentally. But the car roared on by and after it had gone, I saw my dancing girl still behind, still close on our heels, but far enough back to handle.

She was going on with it.

"…don't remember most of the details. I was drunk almost all the time; blind, reeling, crying drunk. When we parted, I think he hated me. I remember bitterness and harsh words. I never saw him again. A month later, he was killed in an automobile accident near Chicago. David never knew who he was—but he knew the child couldn't be his. How well he knew!"

"Please—" I started, but she pressed on.

"Funny—in the beginning, she didn't seem like mine even to me. She began to be mine later, after she was gone. The whole thing was handled with great discretion and secrecy. Masterfully. David took care of every-thing—including the adoption. There were never any recriminations. Only, he wouldn't tell me who had taken her. I saw her as a baby only once, the first day, and I wouldn't have seen her then, except that the doc-tor ordered it over David's objection.

"It took me nine months to find out who had adopted her—a quiet, middle-class couple named Harrison who had enough to take care of her and a history that satisfied the requirements."

I had stepped the speed up to fifty now and the car behind, in true sucker fashion, held to the pace. We had begun to drop down gently from the ridge and the curves were sharper now.

"…I never let her know. I managed to keep myself from telling her. I wangled an acquaintance with the Harrisons and they would invite me to the house. I even did some baby-sitting for them. But I never told her. They were good to her. She loved them. I sent her things—not expensive things—little things they couldn't object to. They never knew who I was any more than she did. I think they liked me. But they wouldn't have liked expensive gifts, nor for me to give the child money. I think Arline liked me too. I really think she did."

It was time for another drink. She offered me one this time and I took it. It helped.

"It happened one afternoon after school. She was walking home with some other children in the neighborhood. The school was only two blocks from the Harrisons' home and it was a quiet, respectable part of town. A car pulled up and a woman leaned out and called—" I looked at her.

"You say, a 'woman' leaned out?"

"The children who were with her said it was a woman." I reached into the back seat, got hold of the blouse with the pearl buttons, pulled it across and handed it to her.

"Does this look familiar?" I said.

She leaned forward, examining the blouse in the light from the dash. It took quite a while. Finally she found a blue mark in the hem. She turned her head slowly and looked at me.

"It's mine," she said. "It's an old one. I haven't worn it for several years. What are these stains on it?"

"I don't know for sure," I said, which was technically true.

I took it from her and tossed it into the back seat. She was staring at me.

"Mac—" she said.

"Excuse me for interrupting."

There was a pause before she went on.

"I didn't know anything about it until I read it in the paper the next day. That's when I cut the clipping I showed you this morning."

"You say that according to the kids with her, a woman leaned out of the car and called her by name. She went to the car—?"

"The others said she went to the car and the door opened and then she was inside and the car was going away. That's all they knew."

"Did they describe the car?"

"They said it was a big black car."

After about half a minute, I said:

"How far ahead would you think this intersection is?" She looked out the window. We were going down a long slope.

"It's at the bottom of the hill," she said.

"Does this main road go straight ahead?"

"Yes—well, there's a curve toward the Lake—it can't be more than five miles—"

"You might want to hang onto something," I said.

She said nothing, but reached out and took hold of the upholstered door pull to her right. My speedometer was at sixty now, but even with the lights on the high beam I couldn't see far enough ahead to find the intersection. The car behind had dropped back some and I gave it some more till we hit seventy. It dropped back again for a few seconds, then began to move up. I slowed to sixty, then to fifty-five and it was right on my tail.

Wide, white letters on the highway read SIGNAL AHEAD. I nosed toward the right shoulder, watching for the stop sign, slowing enough to bring them closer. They came along. There was a red flash, as if he had come too close for comfort and pushed at the brake. But he let up right away. I gave it another spurt then, forcing him to speed up and he fell for that too. I had him where I wanted him now and I let it race the rest of the way down to within twenty feet of the stop sign.

"Hang on!" I yelled at her.

I hit the floor with the brake and we lurched. I held it steady to the near edge of the crossroad that showed light gray in the dark, then twisted the wheel sharply to the right and we skidded onto it, bucking a little as we came to a stop. I had time to see the other car plunge ahead, past the intersection, and I heard the sound its tires made, squealing under the brakes. Then it went out of sight.

"Could you drive a little?" I said.

"Yes, if I have to."

"I'll get out. Take the car slowly to wherever you can turn around, then bring it back, but slowly."

I got out. The motor was still running and we hadn't blown any tires. We were lucky. She slid in where I had been and I closed the door.

"When you come back," I said, "don't get out of the car, no matter what's going on, unless I yell for you."

"All right," she said.

She got it going, a little jerkily, and the lights faded down the narrow country road. There were bushes growing close to the intersection itself and I walked behind them on the side of the road nearer the Lake and got my gun out in my hand. I waited. The lights of the Buick had disappeared now among the trees and it was dark everywhere, with no moon.

I didn't like it that it was such a long wait. But I remembered making the quick turn at nearly forty-five and the other car would have had plenty of momentum. I could see the main road clearly from where I stood in the bushes, and my hand was steady.

It seemed like two or three minutes, but was probably only forty-five seconds, before I heard the sound of a motor. I looked around then, wondering whether she had turned already, but the Buick headlights were nowhere in sight. Then light gleamed faintly on the main road and brightened steadily. The sound was low, so I knew they were crawling. They crawled to the stop sign and pulled up. I could see the two of them in the front seat, but I couldn't tell who they were. I dropped the gun into my other hand, flexed my fingers and put it back where it belonged, where it would do some good.

The car started up slowly from the sign, then bore left and turned into the crossroad toward me. The headlights swung in a wide arc on the opposite side of the road and they never did get a chance to find me. I let them get all the way off the highway. They had white sidewall tires. It was easy. From fifteen feet, I blasted a hole in the left front the. The car bucked and the wheels twisted before he could catch it, but he managed to bring it to a stop and cut the lights.

I stepped out from behind the bushes so they could maybe see the gun.

"Get out of the car," I said, "on this side. Hurry it up and don't play games, because believe me, I'll kill you."

There was some hesitation. I could see the white face of the driver and his hands on the top of the wheel. It wasn't a face I recognized.

I squeezed off and sent a slug into the hood. It ricocheted into the night and made plenty of racket. The door opened and the driver practically fell out, his hands up by his shoulders, his face looking for me. He should have known where to look by this time.

His companion climbed out behind him, bumping into him, so that both of them staggered a little before they got straightened up. Headlights gleamed far down the crossroad and I knew she was coming back, slowly, as I had requested. She was a good, brave girl. She was maybe the one— if there was ever to be one.

But this was no time. The two laddybucks were standing there, waiting for instructions. I still didn't recognize the one who had been driving. But as the Buick headlights brightened, I managed to place his companion. He stood beside the driver, his hands slack, but in plain sight. He was Louis Arvin.

CHAPTER NINETEEN

She drove the Buick slowly and steadily to within about twenty feet of the stalled car and stopped, leaving the lights on. The two chumps in the road were getting edgy. They shifted their feet, glanced toward the Buick, then Arvin looked back at me.

"What's going on?" he said. "What do you want?"

"Relax," I said. "Duchess! Baby!"

The door of the Buick opened and she came diagonally across the road, hesitantly, but with that wonderful poise. Like the smart girl she was, she had left the car lights on.

"Yes, Mac?" she said quietly.

"May I have your hand, please?"

She held out her right hand and I moved the gun into it, holding her index finger carefully out from the trigger guard. After she had a good grip on it, I curled her finger gently and brought it to rest on the trigger.

"We have to be careful," I said so everybody could hear, "because the safety is off and we wouldn't want anybody to get hurt."

Arvin let his nerves get the best of him.

"Look—" he said, "what the hell do you—?"

"Got it, Baby?" I said.

Her voice was small.

"Yes."

"Just hold it so it points at them. If either one of them moves, pull the trigger. Don't ask any questions. Just pull it. Then pull it again."

"All right," she said.

This was the only real tricky part of it. The safety was not off and if she should have to pull the trigger, it wouldn't mean anything. But you couldn't have everything. If anybody was going to do any killing, I couldn't let it be her.

I left her with the gun and went quickly to the car they'd stalled in the middle of the road. I twisted the wheel till it was headed toward the side of the road. I released the emergency brake, went around behind it and started pushing. It took some straining to get it going, but the slope to the side was sharp and once it was rolling, it went right along. There was a shallow ditch and it had enough momentum to carry it on across and into the weeds growing beside the road. It was well out of the way and it would take quite a while to get it going again. I doubted that they could change the tire without hauling it back onto the road.

They were standing meek as kittens, letting her hold the gun on them. I almost laughed at them, but restrained myself. We were still in the tricky stage.

I got between Arvin and the Buick's headlights.

"Hold the gun steady, Baby," I said. "Arvin—come here."

"Huh—?" he said.

"Walk over here. Take it easy, just walk slow."

There was some waiting, but then he turned and walked toward me slowly, his hands hanging loosely at his sides, his head thrust forward a little.

"Maybe you'd feel better if you had your knife out," I said. He hesitated. "Go ahead, Louis, get it out."

He took me up on it. His hand made that flashing cut across his chest. I'd hoped he'd get it out quickly, as I knew he could, but his nerves were too tight. He fumbled. So I kicked him before I'd planned on it. He doubled over, then sat down on the road, holding himself. I heard a faint gasp from the Duchess.

Hold on, kid, I thought. It will get worse before it gets better.

Arvin was sitting with his head sagging, his hands on his belly where I'd kicked him. I knocked his hat off, pulled his head back by the hair and felt around till I found his knife. I stuck it in my pocket and pulled him up to his feet. He couldn't seem to get his breath. He would need his breath for what I wanted. I let him stand there till he found it. Finally he found enough to say, "What—?"

"Where's Stella Perino?" I asked.

His mouth dropped open. He stared at me. Then he shook his head.

I used my fist this time, felt it tear something inside him and jumped out of the way just in time as he vomited, going down. I left him there and went over to the other one, who had turned his head to watch.

"What's your name?" I asked.

"What you want with me—?"

I hit him on the bridge of the nose and he grabbed at it with his hand.

"What's your name?" I said.

There were tears on his cheeks.

"Pete—" he said weakly. "Pete Broda."

"All right, Pete," I said, "lie down on the edge of the road."

He just looked at me. I gave him a push behind the shoulder and he twisted and went down on one knee at her feet. She was staring at me.

"Lie down," I said. "Right there."

He looked up once, but then he stretched out on his stomach and put his face in his arms. I led the Duchess past him and about four feet away from his head and took off my coat. I laid the coat on the edge of the road.

"Sit down, Baby," I said. "Better look at the woods for a while. Some of this may be unpleasant."

She sat down on my coat, drew her legs up under her and arranged her skirt. She was still holding the gun and I got it placed for her, across her lap, aimed at the guy's head.

"Look, Pete," I said.

He raised his head warily to peer toward us.

"If he moves, Baby," I said, "pull the trigger. You can't miss."

There was plenty of light and I knew he knew she couldn't miss. What he didn't know wouldn't hurt him.

I turned back to the road. Arvin was on all fours now, shaking his head back and forth, breathing in gasps. I squatted down in front of him.

"Where's Stella Perino?" I asked him.

He lifted his head and looked into my face. His looked a little gray.

"I don't know," he said. "Honest, I don't know—" I grinned at him.

"Look, Arvin," I said, "I don't mind slugging you. I'd just as soon stand here and kick you in the belly all night long. It would be a pleasure. Only, I've got nothing against Joey and Francie. You tell me where Stella is and I won't hit you again. O.K.?"

"I tell you—" he said, still shaking his head, "I don't—" I hit him on the jaw, lifting. He went all the way over backwards and his head banged on the road. He lifted it, his fingers digging at the macadam, then let it drop.

I went over and looked down at him, nudging him with my foot. He didn't move.

"That one was for Mick Sloane," I said.

I had a moment of doubt. Maybe he didn't really know. I didn't think he had guts enough to take a beating for anybody else—even Mr. Smith.

But he must know. Spig had seen him coming out of Stella's with a suitcase. Spig might have been lying, but probably not, because he'd already known he wouldn't get the money till after he'd delivered the message and got a signature. I thought Spig was probably telling the truth.

I got hold of his coat and pulled him up to his knees. I gave him the back of my hand a couple of times and he blinked and opened his eyes.

"Where's Stella, Louis?" I said.

"She's—all right."

"That's good. But where?"

His head drooped. I slapped him again. He tried to break away from me and I pulled him up closer.

"Where did you take the suitcase you brought out of her place this afternoon?"

He quit blinking and stared at me.

"Where, Louis?"

He opened his mouth a couple of times but said nothing and I made a fist and drew it back slowly to my shoulder. He watched me till I reached the point where I could throw it the hardest and then he cracked.

"She's at—the Grotto," he croaked.

"Where at the Grotto?"

He started to shake his head and I tightened my grip on his coat.

"…cabin—in the back," he said.

I let go of him and he toppled over. He didn't try to get up. I bent over, got his coat again and dragged him across the road to where Pete lay still with his head on his arms.

I went to the Duchess, gave her a hand up, picked up my coat and got it on and took the gun. She stood very still beside me.

"Get in the car," I said.

She walked away and I heard the car door slam. I walked over and nudged Pete with my foot.

"We're leaving now," I said. "Have a nice walk home." He didn't say anything. I went to the Buick, climbed under the wheel and got it going. They were still lying there beside the road as I passed and turned into the main highway leading to the Lake.

She didn't say anything for quite a while. She got out the flask and had a drink and I had one and after a while she said:

"I wasn't quite honest with you. I pretended I could do it all right, with the gun. But I couldn't have, Mac. I couldn't have pulled the trigger."

"I know it. But they didn't know it, so it worked out."

Pretty soon she said, "Did you find out what you wanted to know?"

"Some of it," I said. "I had guessed most of it. But there was more to it than information. That was Joey Arvin's big brother."

"Joey—? The friend of Bill's?"

"Joey thinks his brother is hot stuff. I would like to destroy that illusion."

She was quiet for a while. Then she said, "But Joey wasn't there—"

"That is true. But Louis can't take it much. If he breaks down far enough, there won't be anything left in him to respect—even toughness."

After a few more moments—"Mac—if Joey had been there, watching —would you have done it—the same way?"

"No," I said. "I would have done it differently. It would have taken more time and it would have been less certain. But I would have tried it."

"What about the girl—Stella?"

134

"I don't know."

"Do you think she's in danger? If she participated in that frame-up against you—"

"She participated all right, and I have to find her. But I don't think she's in immediate danger. There's still some use for a girl as pretty as she is."

She said nothing more then. We came to a fork. To our right, the sign read, was Manitou Beach Resort; to our left, North Lake Thomas. And beside that on another post, an ornately carved sign read: The Blue Grotto, with an arrow pointing to the left. I turned onto the Lake road and wound among trees till they thinned, then disappeared behind us and the Lake was on our right, gray and smooth in the dark, and no lights. We passed a few cottages built close to the water, then veered away from the Lake, went up a low hill, wound through more trees, topped the rise and below us, along the shore where it curved in a small bay, were lights, a low rambling building with smaller buildings behind it, some half-hidden in the woods, and a neon sign at the edge of the road, reading: *Blue Grotto.*

"How is the food here?" I asked.

"I don't know," she said. "I was here only once—several years ago. I don't remember how it was."

"We haven't eaten since four o'clock," I said.

"I know, Mac."

I pulled into a gravel parking area in front of the place. There were three or four cars parked there. They would hardly be enough to transport the help. I wondered why they stayed open off season.

135

CHAPTER TWENTY

I turned the Buick around and put it where it couldn't be blocked and where it would be heading in the right direction when it was time to leave. The Duchess got out and I locked all the doors and gave her the keys. She put them in her purse and we walked up the drive, up a wide flight of steps onto a porch that ran the width of the building. There were deck chairs and chaises out there but they looked dirty and worn and as if they had not yet been replaced by the summer furniture.

We entered a large dining room. A flight of stairs led up at one end of the room and at the other end was a curtained archway with a Cocktails sign over it. There were no customers. There were no waitresses in sight either. The tables were all set, but nobody was using them. We stood around for a while and a guy came out of the cocktail lounge, wearing a tuxedo, caught sight of us and bustled over.

"Good evening, sir, madame," he said, cooing it. "Are you having dinner?"

"Can we have it in the lounge?"

"Certainly," he said. "This way, please."

We followed him among the tables, through the archway into a dark, cool cocktail lounge with comfortable booths upholstered in genuine leather. The rest of the appointments were rustic, but expensive and in what seemed to me to be good taste. They probably made money during the season.

We sat down in one of the booths and the maitre d' bustled around for a while, took our cocktail order and disappeared. A very pretty waitress came in, set the table and handed us menus the size of a tabloid newspaper.

"We have everything except the out-of-season items and the roast pork," she said. "The prime ribs are extra good."

I looked at the Duchess and she nodded.

"That will be for us," I said, "rare and with whatever is good to go with it."

The waitress smiled happily and went away. The Duchess finished her cocktail and rose, excusing herself.

"If you're going to the ladies' room," I said, "and if there's an attendant in there and if she's friendly, you might get her into a conversation."

"Anything special I should ask, Mac?"

"Just open her up. Sometimes, if they get going, they'll do a lot of talking before they realize it. They usually don't have much to lose."

"I'll try."

She went away. I admired her till she was out of sight, then got up and went to the bar. I ordered a highball and after he'd brought it, the bartender stood around, drying glassware. He was a well set up guy and the white jacket he wore fit him neatly. He had dark hair, a Latin complexion and he was bored to the point where it was ridiculous.

"Big business tonight," I said.

He shrugged and made a face.

"It's dead till the season starts," he said. "I usually always come down couple weeks early."

"Maybe you get some late customers in here—in the bar."

"Nah. Not this time of year."

"You drive back and forth?" I asked.

"Me? Drive? To that town over there?"

"Oh—you don't live around here then."

"Hell no. I come down from Chicago."

"No kidding," I said. "That's *my* town."

He stopped polishing the glass, set it down, threw the towel down somewhere and leaned forward on the bar, resting on one arm, looking at me as if I were his long-lost brother. When he spoke now I could tell where he came from all right.

"Then you know," he said, his voice low and confidential. "Why—a crummy town like that one—. Jeez! You know how it is—out around the Edgewater Beach—or the Palmer House—or out on the South Shore—*you* know."

"I know."

He looked both ways along the bar and lowered his voice some more.

"And there's always a chick for when you get off. Listen, a girl in Chicago is entirely a different matter from what you find down here—except in the season. When they come in from all around. Last summer, for instance, there was this schoolteacher from way down in the state somewhere—" He thought better of it and quit talking about the schoolteacher.

"Man, I like to die in this place the first couple of weeks."

"Is the summer worth it?"

He shrugged.

"I make pretty good money in the summer—and there's always something to do."

I stabbed with my thumb.

"Those places out in back," I said. "I heard they have cabins out here. You live right here on the place? Does the help live here?"

"Nah! Well, some. You can if you want to. The boss'll rent you a cabin, if you want. But not me. The hell with that. When I get off, I got to go somewhere. I got a little place farther up the Lake, been renting it three years now. Real private."

"What's the boss like?" I said. "All right to work for?" He gave me that confidential look again.

"Listen, there's no good bosses," he said. "There's bad bosses and there's bosses that ain't so bad. But there's no good bosses. A guy was any good to get along with, he wouldn't be a boss."

The maitre d' had been loitering at the curtained entrance and suddenly he stuck his head in. The bartender looked at him without changing his position.

"Those set-ups," the maitre d' said. "You get those up?"

"Yeah, yeah. I got 'em."

"Better check 'em."

The bartender pushed wearily back from the bar, picked up his towel and went back to work on the glasses.

"See what I mean?" he said.

"I see."

I climbed off the stool and he came forward again, glanced carefully toward the curtains and jerked his head slightly. I leaned on the bar.

"You mentioned them cabins," he said. He looked wisely toward our booth. "They don't ordinarily open them up till a couple of weeks. But I can fix it—if you want one—"

"Well, thanks," I said, going along with the sotto voce. "I don't know. It's our first date—"

"I see she's got plenty of class. That's what they cater to. She's really got it. Class."

"You mean they're all vacant now? Just sitting out there with nobody in them?"

"Yeah. Well, there's somebody—some babe in the last one-up in the woods. I see her last night. I figured her for a new waitress or somethin', but I don't see her on the job. She's O.K.—real well made, but young, you know? Jailbait. Man, you got to watch that stuff."

"Uh-huh," I said. "Thanks for the tip. I'll give you a sign if I want one, O.K.?"

"Sure. O.K."

I paid him for the drink, leaving a dollar tip. The waitress had brought water and butter and a dish of radishes and onions and some crackers and

138

my mouth watered. It was hard to wait for the Duchess. Not that she'd have minded, but I guessed I had let the bartender get under my skin with that "class" talk. I felt a little resentful. Clearly, if I had appeared to have "class" too, he wouldn't have spoken so freely about her. So I could only assume that whereas she, the Duchess, Cynthia, Mrs. David Cameron, had class; I, Mac Nobody, had none whatsoever.

But then, if the tips are big enough, you don't have to have class.

She came back and I slid out of the booth and stood till she'd sat down. Then I slid back on the other side and moved around till we were close enough to talk.

The bartender paid no attention. It was as if he'd never seen me before. He was a good man. I wondered whether I could learn to be a bartender, how long it would take, and how much he made on the average, year by year. More than I, I could bet.

"There was an attendant," she said.

"Oh?"

The waitress brought us soup and we waited till she had left.

"She wasn't very talkative at first. I didn't ask her any direct questions. When she did say something, it was mostly about family troubles. She wants to go to California. 'Us folks get along better out there,' she said. I'm afraid I didn't learn much."

She ate some of the soup.

"But then," she said, "just as I was leaving, she called me back and got very confidential."

"Yeah?"

"She said—" She broke off and ate some more of her soup.

"Well?" I said.

"She said—" her face was turned from me, but I could see it flushing. "Well, she offered to 'fix me up,' as she put it—with one of the cabins— for tonight. She said they don't ordinarily open them up till the season starts. 'But honey—' she said—"

"All right," I said. "You want to know something?"

"What, Mac?"

"You've got class. Capital C class."

She stared at me across the soup tureen.

"What are you talking about?"

I grinned at her.

"Nothing," I said. "Wouldn't it be nice if this were our first date, and nothing more, and that all we had to do was have this dinner and then go for a moonlight ride on the Lake and then drive slowly back to town and just take it easy and—"

"Could we pretend it's that way, Mac?"

"No. It wouldn't help. It's not that way and I'm sorry. But, for one thing, I'm an inquisitive type—" I found her free left hand under the table and squeezed it hard. I held it until she had registered an alert and then I let go and went on with the soup. But it dropped thinly into my stomach and I felt the dream break in a silent rending of fine tissue, like cobwebs, because a guy had come through the curtains and taken a seat at the bar, and although he had not seen me, I had ample opportunity to examine him.

He looked immaculate and well cared for and perfectly at ease, the thin one, the gray man in the gray suit—the man I'd had a drink with while Beasly stalled for time.

CHAPTER TWENTY-ONE

He didn't look around any, just sat there at the bar with his back to the room and the bartender brought him a long drink. They didn't have any conversation.

The waitress brought our meal and we got pretty far into it in a short time. I couldn't tell for certain whether he had seen us or not. There was a mirror behind the back bar, but from his angle, I doubted that he could have seen either of us in the booth.

I didn't see how he could have missed seeing the Buick in the parking lot—if that would mean anything to him.

It would have to mean something. He was thick with Beasly. I'd seen that.

He finished his drink and got up. I didn't like that. I'd have preferred to keep him in sight. But it was no time to get up and follow him. I let the waitress take our things and bring coffee and tried to contain myself while we drank it.

"What was it, Mac?" she asked.

"Some guy came in."

"Someone you know?"

"Not intimately. When you're through with your coffee, I'd like you to take a seat at the bar, if you don't mind, and I'll excuse myself for a while."

"Mac, darling—"

"Got to," I said. "You'll be all right in here."

"It's not that—" She finished her coffee and we got out of the booth. She walked with me to the bar and climbed onto a stool. The bartender gave me a long deadpan and I shook my head at him. His expression didn't change. She ordered a highball and he went to make it for her. I took one of her hands.

"I'm sure you'll be all right," I said. "You have the keys to the car. If anything bothers you—anything at all-get in the car and go away. Don't worry about me, just go."

"I couldn't."

"You'll have to, Duchess."

141

I squeezed her hand, straightened my hat on my head and went out into the dining room. It was no busier than it had been when we'd come in, which is to say, there were no customers whatsoever.

I had been stalling around about finding Stella, because I'd hoped that patience and a little judicious snooping might produce an easy way. But the appearance of the gray man had made me think time had run out. I crossed the floor of the dining room and glanced out the front door. I saw nobody on the porch. The maitre d' approached and asked whether everything was all right. I said everything was fine and I thought I'd get a breath of air. My companion was still in the cocktail lounge, having a drink and if he had our bill with him, I would be glad to take care of it up to this point. He said that would be perfectly all right, sir. I pushed through the front door onto the porch and took a couple of deep breaths.

A late moon had come up and it made a thin, silver streak across the water. But it wasn't high enough to give much light. I counted the cars in the parking lot and there were neither more nor fewer than there had been after I had parked the Buick. So the slim man had either been here all the time, or if he had driven out from the city, he had parked somewhere out of sight.

I had been making these difficult deductions all by myself in the dark, standing on the front porch, and I began to feel confused and a little put upon. I tried thinking of the Duchess's murdered daughter, but I had never known her. I tried thinking of Bill Denton, as I had found him on the floor of the slum kitchen, but I could no longer remember what he had looked like nor the sound of his voice. I thought of Joey and Stella and I thought, What's the use? I could go back and get the Duchess and we could leave here and drive to Chicago, where I could turn in the rented car to another agency and maybe life could turn out to be a great and wonderful thing.

And then I thought of Dr. Stein, and the way Francie had looked at him after he'd said—what had he said? I couldn't remember that either. Something about curing the whole world.

Well, I couldn't cure the world. And neither could he alone. I wasn't even sure there was a cure.

But if you had a syringe loaded with anti-tetanus and there was a kid in front of you who had just torn his foot open on a rusty nail—would you throw the syringe away, just because there wasn't enough in it for the whole world?

I guessed not.

There was Stella. She might grow up to be somebody's mother. She might be lucky and get to keep her future, whatever it would be.

I guessed you had to try.

I went down the steps, turned to my left and walked along the front of the Grotto toward the northeast corner. It was a short walk. When I got there I stopped and cased the area some. There was an extra, narrower parking lot on the north side of the club, graveled, with a row of posts marking the end of it. Beyond the posts was a flagstone walk, rising in a gentle slope and beyond that, a row of modern front cottages, set at some distance apart, rising with the slope. They looked comfortable and convenient. Probably went for thirty dollars a night during the season. But they wouldn't put up the help in places like that.

I crossed the parking lot, climbed over the chain and got onto the flagstone. All the cottages were clearly vacant. Papers and refuse had blown against the front walls, and grass plots in front were untended. I walked along the flagstone path, picking my way carefully in the dark, and came to the end of the row.

I'm always coming to the end of something, I thought.

The flagstone dropped off onto a dirt path that wound back and upward from the Lake through a grove of trees. I followed it, moving faster now and once in a while I had to push a branch out of the way. The night air was cold. The back of my right hand was stiff and raw from the way I'd used it on Louis Arvin. I hoped I wouldn't have to use it any more.

The dirt path circled in a wide arc through the grove. To my right I could make out the winding gray ribbon of the road that curved in front of the Grotto, circling toward the north and from which, no doubt, there would be a service drive leading to the rear.

I came across it suddenly as the path gave out and I was looking across a wide, graveled drive that swept in from the Lake road toward the L-shaped rear of the main building.

A couple of cars were parked not far from the kitchen. Beyond them, dimly, I could see the dark shape of a long, low building that looked like a garage.

There were lights inside the Grotto and a dim, yellow bulb over the service door to the kitchen. There were dimmer lights off to the side where the cocktail lounge occupied the wing. A guy in a white cap came out of the kitchen and dumped something into a trash can, lit a cigarette and puffed on it, threw it away and went back inside. There was nobody else in sight.

I started across the service parking lot. There were footsteps on gravel and I ducked and made a quick, silent run for the trees. I made cover all right, but I never did find out who made the footsteps. I heard the kitchen door squeak open and bang shut. I began making my way through the trees, up the hill, keeping the long, low garage on my left as I climbed.

There was no path now and I had to fight my way through branches and over rough growth on the ground. By the time I reached a cleared area higher up, I was panting.

I looked around, wishing the moon were bigger or that somebody would turn on a light, and finally I saw more buildings back among the trees. They were no doubt the cabins the bartender had referred to as reserved for the help. They were small and rustic and wouldn't have much of a Lake view. They wound up the hill into the woods in a ragged curve. I beat my way through the foliage to the nearest of them.

Nobody home there. It was boarded up and the padlock on the door was buried in cobwebs. I had found another path now and the going was easier. I passed two more locked cabins, then none for twenty yards and then there were three, in a line curving off to the left. Because of the way they were set, I didn't see the lights in the third one till I was right on top of it. I saw them suddenly and although the illumination wasn't blinding, it was a shock. I jumped off the path into the bushes.

The light was behind drawn curtains, but it was bright light and made quite a glow in the dark. There was a big window on the front and a smaller one in the near end and the curtains completely covered both of them. Behind the main room was a projection that probably enclosed a bath.

The shrubbery grew close all around and I made a path through it slowly, lifting my feet high. Still it crackled some. I got to the projection at the rear of the cabin. There was a window in it and the curtain had not been drawn, but there was no light on in the bathroom.

It was small, with a stall shower. The door was partly open and through the opening I could see some of the main room of the cottage. A double bed took up most of the space. There was a straight chair beside it and a floor lamp with a bright bulb. On the bed was an open suitcase. I waited, watching, and after a couple of minutes a girl came in sight, carrying some lingerie, which she dropped into the suitcase.

It was Stella, all right, fully dressed and evidently steady on her feet, with her pretty face made up and her pretty, still young, fresh figure artfully revealed under what must be a brand-new dress. They were giving her quite a sendoff.

Beside the projecting bath was a screen door over an inner wooden panel. I pulled on the screen door lightly. It squeaked some, but by lifting as I pulled, I got it open without much sound. I tried the knob of the wooden door, but it was firmly locked. I let the screen door back silently.

The voice spoke from about eight feet behind me, low and gentle.

"Stand still, shamus," it said.

I stood quite still.

"We're going in there," it went on, "so you won't have to be a Peeping Tom—not that you aren't used to it."

I waited. It came again.

"Start walking," he said. "Walk as I count and don't do anything unusual. Nobody here, including the D.A., cares much about you any more. I've got a big gun in my hand and I know how to use it. Don't think I won't."

I believed him. He knew exactly what to do and he knew I would do exactly as he ordered. So I went, as he had directed, slowly along the back of the cabin to the corner, where he circled wide, giving me no chance to duck out of sight. I passed the lighted side window, went around to the low stoop, climbed up and approached the front door. He called out:

"Open up, Stella! It's Slim."

I heard a bolt slide back, the door open. I heard his quick step behind me, but it was too quick and there was no time to move. I felt the horrible crash on the back of my head, felt myself stumbling and falling into the brightly lighted room. It felt as if he went on clubbing me for a long time, but I think now it was only the savage throbbing in that split second before I passed out.

CHAPTER TWENTY-TWO

I was lying on the floor against the front wall on my back, and my elbows felt as if they had been clamped in a vise for a week. I felt steel biting at my wrists and knew the reason for the bad elbows was that I was lying on them and had been—for how long I didn't know, but it wouldn't have to be long.

My face was turned to the wall and my neck ached. I turned my head slowly to ease it, wincing at the throb in the back where he'd slugged me. I got it past the bad spot, twisted it the rest of the way and saw Stella sitting on the bed. I closed my eyes. She had been sitting with her knees crossed and at the moment I'd seen her, she'd been glancing to one side, so probably she didn't know I was awake. She had my gun in her hand and it was pointed more or less at me. I had had time to see that the safety was off. Evidently for Slim, if there was going to be any killing, it would be all right for Stella to do it.

I lay still for a while with my eyes closed and then I opened them and groaned. The gun was up, level and steady in her hand, and she was watching me over it. I tried to grin at her, but it wasn't much of a grin and it drew no response.

I shifted some, trying to ease the strain on my elbows and she said, "Lie still."

"O.K., kid," I said and lay still.

After a while I said, "Where did he go?"

"To have dinner," she said, laughing as if it were quite a good joke.

It made me nervous to hear her laugh. It made her jiggle. The gun could go off.

"What are his plans?" I asked.

She looked at me with considerable amusement.

"You're not very smart, are you, Mr. Donnelly?"

"No," I said, "I guess not. Not as smart as you."

She quit looking amused, but she didn't ask what I meant.

"Where are they sending you, kid?" I asked her. "Chicago?"

"Wouldn't you like to know?"

She was being real teen-age nasty, but I had the feeling that she was glad for some conversation. I would try to make some more of it.

"Chicago," I said. "A great town. Lights—excitement—dice girls—"

"Shut up."

I laughed a little. It sounded hollow even to me.

"Did they describe it for you, kid? How it would be up in the city? Did they tell you all of it? About how they'd pay your way and give you protection and put you in show business, or something—a real, gay, happy life—?"

She was watching me. I saw the gun twitch in her hand and held my breath. Then it steadied and I laughed.

"What's so funny?" she said.

"What's funny is what they didn't tell you, Stella."

I stopped laughing and let her wait for it. She didn't want to ask me, but she wanted to hear about it. I tried to shift my position again, but the gun came up and she warned me. She was pretty good at following directions. I had no way of knowing how soon he'd get back. I wanted to let her wait longer, but maybe we didn't have the time.

"Stella—" I said, "there's only one thing you've got that's any use to them. How long do you think it will last?"

"Don't preach at me!"

So she'd thought of it. Whatever else, she wasn't stupid.

"All right, Stella. But I could tell you stories that would make you sick to your stomach."

"I don't want to hear them."

"I don't blame you. Wait a while and you can live one yourself. Then you can tell it to somebody else, if you can still talk—"

"Shut up!"

"There's something you ought to see, Stella, before you go. It's in my pocket—" She stared at me hard, then glanced at the door.

"What is it?"

"A picture, Stella."

"Hand it to me."

"I can't. I'm locked up, remember? I can't move."

She glanced again at the door.

"It's in my inside coat pocket," I said. "You can reach it all right."

She studied me again and then she stood up, holding the gun steady.

"Do I look dangerous to you, Stella?" I said. "If you haven't got the guts to put your hand in a helpless man's pocket, you'll have a rough time in Chicago."

I don't know how much of it was curiosity and how much was the sudden thought that after all she might get in a little practice, but she came across the room and knelt beside me, holding the gun inches from my head. She stuck her left hand gingerly inside my coat and felt for the pocket.

"That's it," I said.

She hauled out the photo and crawled back, still on her knees. She had to lay it on the floor and pry it with a couple of fingers to get it unfolded. It would have a couple of cracks across it, but she would be able to see it all right.

She was looking at it and I saw the gun droop suddenly in her hand and heard her quiet indrawn breath.

"That was a little girl named Arline Harrison," I said. "They found her in a trash can not far from where you live. It didn't last long for her, did it?"

She looked a little sick. She turned her face away and for the first time, there was no threat from the gun. Even if she should pull the trigger, it would go wide by three feet. Her face was white under the bright rouge.

"The people who are sending you to Chicago," I said, "are the same ones who killed Arline Harrison. And they'll kill you too, Stella, in time. Maybe by other methods, although if you get out of line, it might happen the same way."

She was supporting herself on one hand, staring at the floor.

"If you want to string along with them," I said, "it's up to you. I can't stop you. But you ought to know."

She made no answer. I hoped she was thinking it over, but I couldn't tell. If I was still just a jerk to her, then it probably wouldn't cut any ice. What did I have to offer?

She realized suddenly that the gun was aimless in her hand. She straightened on the floor and pointed it at me again. Her pretty face was confused and her bright red mouth quivered.

"No," she said. "There's nothing I can do about it."

I looked at her hard and straight.

"I found something you might like to have, Stella."

She didn't change her position. She watched my face.

"You wrote down the license number of the car that picked up Bill Denton. You wrote it on the cover of a matchbook and I found it."

Her mouth opened and closed. She continued to stare at me.

"I don't know why you did it," I said, "but I found it. It's in a safe place and if I don't show up in the next couple of hours, it will be turned over to the police."

Her eyes were squinting at me, as if the light were too bright, or as if she had a sudden pain inside her head.

"They can find you in Chicago, too, Stella."

It was almost as if she had gone into a trance. Her lips moved and I didn't hear the words for several seconds.

"So—what?"

If you have any personal magnetism, Mac, I thought, use it now. All of it.

I looked squarely into her eyes.

"We might make a deal," I said.

She looked back at me, straight across now.

"What?" she said.

"I will see that you get safely back to town. I will give you the matchbook with the license written on it. I won't tell anybody about it. I'll see that you get police protection as long as you need it. You'll have to tell the D.A. what you know, but you haven't committed any crime that he cares about and I'll put in a good word for you. I'll do all this, if you'll promise to go back home and finish school and try to keep your nose clean."

She heard me out, she stared at me for a few moments after I'd finished. Then she looked at the door.

"What if he comes back—?"

"He doesn't have to, Stella, if we move fast enough. Will you do it?"

She gave in all at once and all over. She dropped the gun on the floor. She was beside me on her hands and knees and she was good and scared.

"Yes," she said. "I will. I'll do anything."

It was the truest statement she'd made so far.

"Do you have the key to these handcuffs?" I said.

"No. He threw it out."

"Threw it—?"

"He said nobody would ever need it again."

"All right. Help me sit up."

She pulled on my arm and I managed to sit up. My elbows screamed at the change in position, heat surged through them and finally they began to tingle. My hands were nearly numb. I flexed my fingers trying to get the circulation started again. She watched me closely.

"Pick up the gun," I said.

She picked it up, half-afraid now, as if it were a new thing to her.

"If he should come back," I said, "could you shoot him?"

She stared at me, shook her head slowly.

"No—I don't think so."

"All right. Maybe he won't come back."

I rolled to one side, spread my legs and caught myself on my knees. I straightened my back stiffly and got to my feet. The handcuffs cut into my wrists in back and I shook my arms, trying to ease that stiffness in my elbows. Even my legs were stiff. I stamped around on the floor and they held me up all right.

"Close the bathroom door," I said.

She did it.

"We'll go out," I said, "and cut through the woods to the Grotto. I'll go first and you'll follow me. All right?"

She nodded, glancing at her suitcase on the bed.

"You'll have to leave that. I'll see that you get some new clothes."

She was still holding the gun and she looked down at it with a kind of curiosity.

"Put it inside my coat," I said. "There's a holster in there."

She pulled back the lapel of my coat, reached in with the gun and dropped it home. She was almost shy about it.

"Let's go," I said.

I headed for the door. There were footsteps outside. I could hear them against the ground. He hadn't got to the porch yet. I backed quickly, bumping into her.

"Get out a lipstick," I said.

She dug in her purse, came up with a lipstick.

"Rub it on my forehead, quick."

She did it.

"Get the gun again."

She reached in and yanked it out. The footsteps sounded on the porch and I let myself down to the floor. I whispered to her loudly.

"Tell him you had to shoot me. Then just get back out of the way."

Somehow she got the lipstick out of sight and backed as far as the bed before he opened the door. I had flopped onto my back again near the wall and closed my eyes. It was all up to her now. She would have to carry it. The lipstick might look real enough for long enough. I lay still, trying not to breathe, fighting the impulse to open my eyes. I heard the door close quietly.

"Well—?" I heard him say.

"I had to shoot him!"

She said it in a rush, as if it were all one word.

"You—what?"

His footsteps were light and quick across the floor.

"I had to shoot him. He—"

I felt him beside me now, the slight warmth of his body. He didn't touch me and I couldn't be certain of his position. I held on, still holding my breath.

He was closer now, his knee scraped against my ribs as he knelt. I began to count, one, two, three—I felt his hand on my head, in my hair. I opened my eyes wide and he was right over me—ten inches from my face. I pushed up from the shoulders hard, bending my head forward.

It was a solid connection with his chin. The impact nearly knocked me out again. But it nearly knocked him out too. He fell back away from me, kicking with his feet. I rolled onto my knees, sucking for breath. He had fallen against the bed and he pushed away from it with one hand, coming back at me. I dived from the knees, butting him in the stomach with my head. He fell back again and I twisted, got my feet together, rolled over and kicked at him. It caught him in the neck and he grabbed the place. There was a wrenching pain in my right elbow from the twisting. I waited long enough to get my eyes in focus and he was still on the floor, squirming a little. I kicked at his head and he rolled to get out of the way. I got onto my knees and pushed up to my feet, got my balance and jumped on his chest. When he tried to grab my ankle, I jumped off, nearly fell and stumbled back, measuring the distance as I went. He was still kicking, turning his head, trying to find me. I pulled back my right foot and let him have it in the head. It sounded like a rock hitting a pumpkin. He lay still.

I leaned against the wall beside the door, getting my breath back. There was some pain in my right elbow, but my hands and arms had come back to life. I looked at Stella, who was staring down at him. She still had the gun in her hand.

"Put the gun back," I said.

She came over and put it away. I jerked my head at the door. She opened it and I stepped out onto the stoop. There was nobody in sight.

"We'll go this way," I said. "Better turn off your light and close the door."

She did it. I went down off the porch and heard her following close behind. We got into the woods right away and I made my own path down toward the Lake. The brush was thick and hard to walk through and once she fell. I kept going and heard her catch up with me. She was panting now with the exertion and once I heard her sob. We got to the point where the Lake road in front of the Grotto curved away from the water. There was nobody between us and the building and it looked like a good time.

I led her away from the trees, cutting toward the road. After we got into the clear, she stepped up beside me. The Grotto was fifty yards ahead and across the road. The moon was brighter now. We made for the near corner of the porch. There was light on the porch, but the side of the building was in deep shadow. At the corner of the porch I stopped and looked across the parking lot toward the road. The Buick sat where we had left it.

Stella had gone on when I stopped. She looked around and retraced her steps.

"Inside, in the cocktail lounge," I said, "there's a woman with silver hair. Tell her your name. Tell her we have to go back now and that I'm waiting at the car. If you tell her you are Stella Perino and that Mac is waiting, she'll come."

She looked at me in the dark.

"Mac?"

"That's right."

She turned away and went along the porch, up the steps and inside. I took a glance around and crossed the parking lot to the Buick. I went around it to the dark side and leaned against the front door, breathing slow and deep.

It seemed like forever. I waited and waited and after an endless time, I heard the front door of the Grotto bang. I was afraid to look. I stood against the car, waiting. Footsteps crunched on the gravel of the parking lot. There were two sets of them. I waited.

She came around the back of the car, saw me and stopped dead. The moonlight glinted on her silver hair. She stood for maybe ten seconds, staring, then she ran, stumbling on the gravel.

"Mac!" she said.

"Sorry," I said. "I forgot about the bill."

Her face was against my chest, her hands on my arm.

"Hey," I said, "stiffen up. We have to go. Quick."

She pushed back away from me.

"You'll have to drive," I said.

"All right," she mumbled. "All right."

She was fumbling in her purse for the keys and I saw Stella move up behind her, slowly, watching us. When she found the keys, she tried to hand them to me and I twisted, showing her the handcuffs.

"No!" she said.

"Yeah. Unlock it, Baby. Front and back."

"But, Mac—"

"You can drive, can't you?"

"I guess so. I've been in there, at the bar—"

"You can do it."

She got the front door open and reached around to pull up the lock on the back.

"Get in, Stella," I said.

She climbed into the back seat and I got in beside her.

"Sorry to make you do all the work," I said to the Duchess. "We can go now."

She climbed in under the wheel and got it started.

"Back to town?" she said.

"That's right."

She started off. The car jerked, starting, and I knew she wasn't used to driving. I sat in the back seat, leaning against the cushions, with Stella beside me, rigid and silent, and after we got onto the road and straightened out, she drove along all right. I watched her silver hair in the moonlight.

CHAPTER TWENTY-THREE

We got along fine at first. She drove fast and straight and there was no traffic in either direction. But she was leaning forward in the seat and I could tell by the way she gripped the wheel that she was tense and hated having to drive. We'd gone three or four miles when she spoke up.

"Isn't there some way we can get those things off you?"

"Not till we find a locksmith," I said. "If you want to stop for a minute, go ahead and stop."

"I'm all right," she said.

It was hard sitting with my hands behind me and I shifted so that I could lean against the seat with my shoulder, with one knee up on the seat. That fixed it so all I had to look at was Stella. She wasn't hard to look at except that I kept wondering, What will happen to her?

And I didn't want to care.

But I didn't have all the information yet. Maybe she had softened up enough to let me have it.

"Who paid you to pose for those pictures in my apartment?" I asked her.

No answer. She looked straight ahead.

"Who was it, Stella?"

She turned her head a little, but wouldn't look at me.

"Louis Arvin," she said.

"How much did he give you?"

"A hundred dollars."

"Didn't that seem like a lot?"

She shrugged.

"Louis Arvin wouldn't have a hundred dollars of his own, would he?"

"No."

"Where do you suppose he got it?"

"I don't know."

I guessed it was possible she wouldn't know that.

"All right," I said, "this is the big one. You might as well practice on it. The D.A. will want to know. Who was with you last night when you went to get Bill Denton?"

Her face flashed toward me, then she moved away, toward the far side of the seat. She was working on her mouth with the fingernails of her right hand.

"Let's have it, Stella," I said.

She looked at me with her white face from the far side of the car. We hit a bump and it was a big one. The car swayed and the Duchess slammed on the brakes, gasping a little at the same time. She kept it under control and we stayed on the road all right, but she was scared now and after we leveled off, we were going very slowly.

"You're all right," I said. "Try to relax."

She didn't answer.

"Stella—?" I said. "I wouldn't ask the questions if it weren't important to both of us."

After a long silence, she said, "Please—Mr. Donnelly—"

"The game is over," I said. "Call me Mac."

"I—Mac?—I didn't know why we were going to get Bill. Honest I didn't know—"

"O.K. Who was with you?"

"Just some of the kids. They picked me up in front of Joey's—"

"Then you didn't stay with Joey till it was time to go home and dress?"

"No. I told him I'd meet him there—"

"All right. Go ahead. They picked you up. Were you expecting them? Was it planned in advance?"

"No. They just stopped out in front and blew the horn and I went down."

"What time was this?"

"I—don't remember—"

"Try to remember."

"It was dark."

"How did you know they wanted you?"

"By the way they blew the horn. There's a certain—"

"All right."

"And I went down and they said we were going to go pick up Bill Denton, to have some fun with him."

"What kind of fun?"

"I didn't know—I thought they were going to bring him to the party."

"Why did they want you to go along?"

"Because—I used to go with Bill. They thought he'd come out if I asked him."

"And he did."

"But I didn't know—I swear, Mr. Don—Mac—I didn't know."

"Who else was in the car?"

She began reeling off names, but none of them meant anything to me.

"Was Louis Arvin with them?"

"No."

"After you picked him up—after he came and got in the car—where did you go then?"

"We drove around for a while, just talking, and then we stopped and there was another car parked at the curb and a woman leaned out and called Bill."

"A woman?"

"It wasn't anybody I knew."

"And Bill got out and got in the other car?"

"Yes."

"Without any objections?"

"Yes. I thought he knew who she was. I didn't think any more about it."

"And that was when you wrote down the license number of the other car?"

"Yes."

"What made you do that?"

"…I don't know."

"Was it because you thought something might be going to happen and if you had a license number you might find out who was in the other car and maybe blackmail her a little?"

There was a long pause.

"I didn't know what was going on," she said softly.

"O.K. What did you do then?"

"We drove back to the party and I met Joey."

"Did you tell Joey about it, after you met him?"

"No. They told me not to. They told me not to tell anybody at all. They said if I told anybody, they'd kill me."

"Who told you this?"

"One of the kids in the car."

"Didn't you think then there was something more to it than just—having fun with Bill Denton?"

"I didn't know! They talk like that all the time."

"They threaten to kill people?"

"Yes, but they hardly ever do."

"Hardly ever?"

"I never heard about them—killing anybody."

"And you don't know who the woman was in the waiting car, the one that called Bill over there?"

"No."

"Could you recognize her if you saw her again?"

"Maybe. It was dark."

I thought it over.

"Then after you left my place—after you posed for the pictures—Louis Arvin picked you up and took you to the Grotto?"

"Yes. He said they were after me and I'd have to hide out."

"Who was after you?"

"Some of the uptown kids—on account of Bill—"

"You believed that?"

"Sure I did. Joey's crowd isn't the only gang in town. Those uptown kids—they've got guns and knives too. They swipe guns from their fathers—"

"All right. When Louis picked you up—first he took you home?"

"Yes. But I was afraid to go in. My mother—"

"So he drove away again and ran into somebody."

Her head jerked as she turned to stare at me.

"No! I don't remember—"

"How did it happen, Stella?"

It took quite a while. When she spoke, her voice was so low I had to lean across the seat to hear.

"We just started up. There was a man coming across the street. He yelled at us. Louis—stepped on the gas. I couldn't—I closed my eyes—"

It was a bad memory for her. It would be bad for a long time.

"Did you know the man was a cop? A detective? That he was coming to see that you were all right?"

She put her face in her hands.

The car lurched suddenly, then came to a full stop. I looked and saw that the Duchess had lowered her head to the wheel, was resting it there. I leaned toward the front seat.

"What do you want me to do?" I asked.

She lifted her head.

"Nothing. I'm sorry. It's just—"

"Can you see the road all right?"

"Yes."

"Does it blank out once in a while?"

"Sometimes."

"Maybe if you just drive along slowly, about thirty, stay well over to the right side—"

"Yes, Mac. I'll try it again."

She got it going. I looked at Stella. She had crumpled down on the seat with her head in her arms. I felt very lonely.

157

Far ahead I saw a pair of headlights approaching. They were coming very fast.

"If you want to, pull over," I said.

"I'm all right," she said.

The lights bore down on us and we began to swerve. It had got her. She was losing control. The gravel of the shoulder grated under us, then for a moment we headed directly into the oncoming lights. There was a screech of brakes and we lurched again and the lights passed us. It was a truck, a good-sized produce truck and it could have smeared us into the bright blue yonder. But she managed to get us stopped on the edge of the shoulder. Even at that, we were heading into the ditch.

She was leaning on the wheel now and her shoulders were shaking. Stella sat straight up in the seat, hanging onto the strap beside the door. I leaned across the back of the seat.

"I've got an idea," I said, "if you'll get out, please."

After a moment she opened the door and got out.

"Will you get my gun out, Stella?" I said.

She looked at me.

"Get it out! You know where it is."

She reached into my coat and pulled out the gun. The Duchess had the back door open and was standing in the road, holding it.

"Hand the gun to her," I told Stella.

The Duchess took it with a trembling hand. I climbed out of the car and she followed me to the front of it, into the light of the headlamps. I bent over, facing her, holding my wrists up as high as I could get them over my back.

"There will be a keyhole there, close to one of my wrists," I said. "Take the gun, hold it right against the keyhole and pull the trigger."

"Mac—I can't—"

"You want Stella to drive?"

"No. But—the gun—"

"You can't hurt me, Baby. The worst you could do would be to crease my fanny and—never mind. Just shoot out the keyhole."

I bent way over, holding my wrists up and straining to keep them apart and after a while she leaned across my back with the gun. I could feel her arm along my spine.

"Get it real close," I said. "We don't want to waste the ammunition."

I felt the muscles in her forearm stiffen. There was a faint metallic click.

"It's touching the keyhole," she said.

"Then let go," I said.

"But, Mac—"

158

"Shoot it, goddam it!" I said.

She did it. There was a hell of a loud report. It felt as if my wrists had been tied to a tree and somebody had run into me with a team of horses. There was a searing burn across my left wrist and the impact knocked me onto my shoulder. But when I could move, my hands were free, one on each side, and except for the burned area on my wrist and a couple of embarrassing bruises, I was all right. Breaking the lock had only opened the one on my left wrist and the cuffs still dangled from the right, but I could use both hands.

I got on my feet and she was standing in front of the car, looking down at the gun with horror. I patted her shoulder and the handcuffs jingled.

"O.K.," I said. "Let's go back to town."

I put the gun away and opened the door. She slid across the seat and I got under the wheel. Stella was sitting upright in the middle of the back seat.

I got the car on the road and we were off. It took the Duchess a long time to relax. We'd gone five miles when I looked in the mirror and Stella wasn't sitting up any more.

"Is she still with us?" I asked.

She looked back.

"She's crying," she said.

"What time is it?"

"Ten o'clock."

I was happy to hear it. Maybe we would yet be in time.

"May I take Stella to your apartment—"

"Of course," she said.

"It might happen you would lose that privacy. You might have to move."

There was a silence and then I felt her hand on my thigh. It lifted suddenly, then came back slowly and lay there, quiet and warm.

"Then I'll move, Mac," she said.

"Good girl."

From then on I just drove the car and she sat quietly, touching me all the time, but lightly and warmly, and by the time we pulled up in front of her studio at ten-twenty, I felt very big and confident.

I helped her out, opened the rear door and Stella was still crying, sprawled on the back seat. She stumbled out of the car and the Duchess guided her up the walk and up the long stairs to the studio. Inside, I checked through the place rapidly and found it as we had left it. Stella was standing in the middle of the studio, swaying, trying to stop crying. I got out my wallet, found the match cover and handed it to her.

"This is what I promised I'd give you," I said.

159

She stared at it, crumpled it in her hand and closed her eyes. The Duchess led her along the hall back to the bedroom. She was gone half a minute, then came back, closing the door. We met in the middle of the hall. Her eyes were luminously green in the dark.

"I'll be gone for a while," I said. "I think you'll be all right here. You've already used this gun once and you've got the feel of it. I'm leaving it with you."

"No. I—"

"Here, take it."

She took it.

"I say I think you'll be all right. But there's been a lot going on lately and you can never be sure. I want you to make me a promise—the way you promised not to touch that broken glass."

She looked up at me and her green eyes were clear and honest.

"Yes?"

"If you have any trouble—if anybody should come tearing in here with a loud voice, or a threat—I want you to use the gun. Your life may depend on it and that makes some difference to me."

"All right, Mac. Anything else?"

I had already started toward the door. I looked back at her.

"Well," I said, "you might get into something comfortable."

She smiled that wonderful, reluctant, slow smile. I left her and went out of the apartment, down to the car. It was ten-thirty and the night was cool and quivering around me.

Proper procedure would have had me first at a phone, calling for some help. But it was late. I had helped send one good cop to his grave and it was not Clark's job, nor Dr. Stein's. It was just mine. I would have to try it alone.

CHAPTER TWENTY-FOUR

As I got closer to Joey's neighborhood, it grew plain that they had extra cops out. But they were mostly in squad cars, cruising, and I remembered that in this town they had few foot patrolmen and most of them in the quiet areas. Anything breaking out in the streets could be handled. But what if it didn't start in the streets? What about the part they couldn't see from a car, even with their fancy spotlights?

I drove slowly past the saloon where Francie worked as a waitress. I slowed and nearly stopped, then went on. Sometime I could get straightened out with Francie. It wasn't me she had been against. It was fear and insecurity and pushing around.

I cruised past the front of the apartment building where they'd had the party and it was dark. I went on to the corner, turned, turned again and came back along the next street. The alley entrance at that end was midway along the block. I nosed into it and turned off the lights. There was some light showing through the windows of the tenements that flanked the alley and down toward the next street, light showed feebly from the service entrance to the apartment.

Fifty feet short of the service door, I pulled up and set the brake. I couldn't have gone much farther anyway, because there was a truck drawn up opposite the door and no room to pass it. I guessed the squad cars hadn't got around yet to prowling the alleys.

I opened the door silently, got hold of the dangling handcuffs on my right wrist to keep them quiet, and walked on tiptoe toward the door, staying close to the wall. They would have the entrance covered certainly, if they were still in there, and the truck made me think they were. The truck was a converted half-track, with a top added and a bench along each side. It was empty now.

I went on along the wall, grazing it now and then with my shoulder. The door was closed and light showed under it in a thin line. I tiptoed past it, flattened against the wall beside it and let the handcuff dangle free. I stuck out my left foot and kicked at the door with my heel. Then I waited.

I waited for a count of five and then there was some scratching on the inside of the door and the creak of hinges. More light spilled into the alley. I pressed back against the wall and he stuck his head out slowly, looking first straight ahead. There was a gun in his hand and I could see it protruding blackly straight out from his belt buckle. I had hoped he would look out farther, but there was no more time to wait in. He would see me as soon as he shifted his eyes.

I swung my wrist out and up and slammed the dangling bracelets into the top of his head. The gun jerked in his hand, but stayed silent and he fell back inside. I hadn't hit him hard enough to cool him and I twisted past the edge of the door and got inside as he started up with the gun in his hand. I hit the gun with my knee, forcing it up and out of his hand. He swung on me once and I blocked it with my arm and slugged him as hard as I could in the side of the face. He went down and I picked up the gun, tapped him on the head with it and he didn't move. I went on through the door into the kitchen, carrying the gun. There was no sentry in there. I didn't think we'd made enough noise to attract attention from below, and the bedroom door stood open. The lamp was on in there and I saw nobody standing around.

The bed had been pulled out from the wall—or had never been replaced since my visit the night before—and I saw light around the edges of the closed trapdoor. I looked at the gun in my hand. It was about my size and I slid it into my holster.

I got down on one knee and reached for the brass ring in the trapdoor. It came up quietly enough and the light from below flooded into my face, blinding me. I eased the door down silently till it came to rest and leaned there on one knee, looking down. Nobody spoke. Nobody yelled. Nobody shot me and they had no guard posted within sight.

The next part would be tricky and I timed it in advance, going over it carefully. I caught hold of the jingling handcuffs again, sat down on the edge of the hole and swung my legs over and down onto the lowest step I could reach. It wasn't far down and two quick steps would get me to the floor, but I would be in plain sight for a couple of seconds.

The steps made no sound under my feet. I raised up, holding to the edge of the hole with one hand and went on down. I nearly lost my footing, reaching for the floor, but caught myself in time and made for the partition with the "Boys' Club" plaque on it.

I couldn't stick my head around the edge of the partition without being seen and I moved back along it looking for a peephole. The old wood had dried and cracked and there were some knotholes. The knotholes were all above my head, but I found a place where the seams had split and by putting my eye to it I got a view of most of the clubroom.

The voice I had heard from above was droning on, scratchy and monotonous and it could only be coming from the loudspeaker on the wall. I looked up there. They had replaced the "Mr. Smith" seal, but without removing the knife. No doubt they had turned that into a threat from the up-town gang too.

"...the time is almost here," the voice was saying portentously, "when you who fight for Mr. Smith will have the opportunity to get back your own! You have heard the routes pointed out. You have heard the orders of the Lieutenants. You know where to go and what to do..." There was a dramatic pause. "And you know *why!*"

I heard mumbling, scraping of feet, a few coughs. There were about twenty kids in the room, most of them Joey's age. Two or three were older. A few were from my baseball squad. They were sitting on the folding chairs in odd, awkward positions, straining at the words and tense with the need for action. Their faces looked white and drawn in the bright white light.

Behind the long table, in the middle high-backed chair, sat Joey Arvin and on each side of him sat one of the two I presumed were the "Lieutenants." They were not kids. They were Louis Arvin's age. One of them I had seen before in the cigar store. The other was not known to me. Joey sat stiffly straight in the chair, his face even whiter than those of the others, with that lock of black hair falling across his forehead. He wore no bandage and I could see the ugly bruise near his eye.

The voice was rasping through the loudspeaker.

"You will get in the truck. You will be armed. You will be taken to the designated point and you will get out of the truck and take up your positions. On a signal from the Lieutenants, you will advance to the scene of the so-called party that is now in progress. You will enter by pairs by a rear entrance and you will seize those whom the Lieutenants indicate and take them back to the truck. You will find out where they have hidden Stella Perino, using whatever methods are necessary to get the information. And when you have found Stella Perino, you will bring her home and return to this room."

Another of those dramatic pauses.

"You will do all this because if you do not do it, Stella Perino will die and they will charge you falsely with that crime, just as they have with the murder of Bill Denton." Pause. "And you know who killed Bill Denton. Didn't Louis Arvin tell you? Think that over. Think how you were fooled by a man who posed as your friend, as a fine, upstanding athletic coach who only wanted to help you."

I felt my left hand sliding slowly over the rough surface of the partition. My fingers on the dangling bracelet were taut and pinched.

The voice was booming now.

"And this so-called friend killed Bill Denton, God knows for what foul reasons, and left you to take the rap for it, knowing the law will always be ready to believe the worst of you."

There was some more rumbling, more scraping of feet. Somebody growled a curse.

"And not only that!" the voice boomed on. "He tried to seduce your own Stella Perino—you saw the pictures! This was the man who called himself your friend!"

He had them going now. There was a low kind of roar and chairs were being pushed back on the floor. Joey sat with one arm on the table, looking down at it out of his white face. He reached up and brushed the hair back off his forehead, but it fell down again.

About half the kids in the room were standing now, ready to move, but waiting for the word, and Joey sat stiffly at the table.

I moved along the partition, took a deep breath and walked into the brightly lighted room. I walked briskly past the first row of chairs till I stood squarely in front of Joey Arvin.

There were several seconds of dead silence. Maybe the surprise, maybe that plus the audacity of the sudden appearance. The voice had started in the speaker again, but a roar drowned it out. Joey had half risen in his chair and was leaning across the table, staring at me.

"Hi, Joey," I said.

The two Lieutenants were standing up, looking at each other across the top of Joey's head. The crowd in the room had surged forward, but stopped six or eight feet from me. They were making plenty of noise now. I raised my hand with the dangling handcuffs and pointed to the plaque on the wall. They quieted down some. The voice was droning on but the words weren't clear. I spoke loudly above the sound.

"So that's the voice of Mr. Smith!" I said.

The voice stopped immediately. So they had a two-way set-up. They heard what was said at this end too.

I looked at the front rank of kids.

"You know where it comes from? It's hooked up to a cheap microphone in Herman Beasly's back office."

I looked at Joey. His mouth was open, crooked and pink in his white face.

"What you want?" he said. "You're crazy—"

"I want to get some things straightened out," I said. I looked around at them again. "You are the freshest batch of sucker material I've seen in a long time." Somebody growled. One of the Lieutenants stuck his hand out and yelled,

"Get him!"

There was a surge toward me again and I faced them and held up both hands. They hesitated and one of them yelled:

164

"What you want here?"

I showed him my back and looked at Joey.

"For Francie's sake," I said to him quietly, "will you listen?"

He looked at the two Lieutenants, then back at me. Then he sat down in the chair with his arms on the table.

"Hurry it up," he said. "We ain't got much time—"

"You've got plenty of time, Joey. I wish I had the time you've got."

"What you talking—?"

I raised my voice.

"Bill Denton tried to tell you what you were up against," I said, "and he got cut to pieces for his trouble. I didn't kill him, and you know it damned well, Joey. He got cut to pieces for other reasons too and you don't know anything about that. But he tried to tell you." There was another growl from the crowd and I swung around and snarled a shut up. They shut up.

"I'm going on the level with you," I said. "I'm no schoolteacher. I'm a shamus. I came out of the same world you did. The same smells, the same dirt, the same blind alley. I've seen punks like those two hot shots up there behind the table—I've cut them up and eaten them for dinner. I'll do it again."

The tough talk was something they understood. They listened. I didn't know how long it would last. Joey was leaning on his arms, watching me closely. There was no readable expression on his face.

"Suckers," I said, "every one of you, taking orders from a fat ward heeler named Beasly. Hustling up whatever he wants—and for what? For nickels! Listen—any of you know how much long green was picked up last year—for hot cars, furs, reefers, white stuff—in this town alone? You know how much?"

They were still listening.

"Five million bucks!"

They looked at each other.

"Five million bucks," I said. "Enough to keep every one of you guys for the rest of his life without lifting a finger. How much did you get out of it? How much?" The loudspeaker cut in again. The voice was different now, scratchier, maybe even a little hysterical.

"You going to stand there and listen to him?" it snarled. "This is the man who posed as your friend. Full of talk, isn't he? You going to stand there like a Sunday School class and hear lies—" He had them again. They were a little confused, but they'd been waiting a long time. They would have to jump somebody and it might as well be me.

Then there was a sudden sound at the table and I saw Joey standing up, staring toward the steps. A shadow fell across the entrance, past the edge of the partition, and moved into the room.

We all looked at the same time, me from the narrowing aisle between the rank of kids and the long table, Joey and the two Lieutenants from behind the table. We all looked and it was Louis Arvin, with a knife in his hand. He was looking only at me.

He was a mess. His clothes were torn and his pants legs wet around the ankles. His face was twisted out of shape. He couldn't stand straight, he drooped in the middle. But his arm was good enough to hold the knife. When he spoke, his voice was hollow and shaky.

"Get out of the way," he said. "He's mine."

The crowd moved back some, staring. He had the knife up now. There were twenty feet between us—not far for me, but a long, long trip for Louis.

He stood there, trembling, making fists, glaring at me, and finally he charged. He charged down the middle of the aisle toward me and I set myself and waited.

And then he stopped—six feet short of me—crouching, still mouthing, with his left eye twitching rapidly.

"Come on, Louis," I said. "You want to go around again?"

He stayed where he was. I looked at Joey.

"He looks great, doesn't he?" I said. "A real hot shot. You know how he came to look like that?"

Joey stared at his brother and his face, if possible, was whiter than before.

"You've got a choice now, Joey," I said. "You can take him home and nurse him and try to find out how he got to be such a big shot—or you can listen to me make a speech. I hate to make speeches, but I'll try it once more."

He went on staring at Louis.

"These are the dead ones." I counted on my fingers. "Arline Harrison, a little girl, found in a trash can on Grand Avenue six months ago. Bill Denton, found right upstairs here—last night. Number three—a cop named Mick Sloane, run down and killed on Twelfth Street early this morning. These were murders. The cop was murdered by Louis Arvin, a hit-and-run driver who lost his head. The first two were killed for other reasons." I pointed to the plaque high on the wall. "Mr. Smith knows who did it and why. Mr. Smith used you for cover. You had a big fight with the uptown crowd the day after they found Arline Harrison, remember? Mr. Smith arranged it. Mr. Smith had to have cover.

"And he'll let you take the rap for it—you, Joey Arvin. Because you're only a stooge around here. You don't run this gang. You never did. You just listen to the orders and repeat them and that's all the use you are—to Mr. Smith or anybody."

He had taken his eyes off Louis now and was looking at me.

"That's the road to nowhere, Joey. You can't even get to be like Al Capone that way. Al Capone called his own shots. They finally caught up with him, but he called them as long as he could hold on.

"Look at the pictures, Joey—on the walls. There are fighters up there —there's Babe Ruth. Some of the fighters were pretty good. They made it the hard way. So did the Babe.

"And then there's DiMaggio—real great—maybe the greatest of all."

He was looking straight at me now.

"You've got a choice, Joey. You've got the natural talent. You can make up your own mind. But you better do it quick. You think you're going to take your gang uptown and rescue Stella from a fate worse than death."

His eyes snapped at me.

"A fool's errand," I said. "Stella won't be there. I know where Stella is. She's safe and sound and I'll take you to her whenever you're ready."

It was very quiet now. From high up on the wall, there was a rasp of static, a sudden click, as if they had turned off the gadget. My eyes were on Joey's and his on mine, as if we'd locked them together and couldn't pull them apart. I pointed to Louis Arvin, still crouched, impotently furious, on the floor.

"Make up your mind, Joey," I said. "Who do you want to be like? Which will it be? Louis Arvin—or Joe DiMaggio?"

He stood there for maybe half a minute. His eyes swung away from mine and rested briefly on Louis. Then he sank back into his chair and looked straight ahead. I had never lost so hard.

The crowd behind me had had enough talk. Somebody yelled:

"He's nuts! We got the orders—let's go!"

I heard them heading across the room, pulling open the doors of the cabinets along the wall. I heard the clink of the knives and the guns banging against each other. One of the Lieutenants finally found his voice.

"What about him?" he yelled, pointing at me. "You going to let him get away with it?"

That roar came again. I heard the feet coming. They were ready. They'd been built up to it and nothing was going to take it away from them. I threw Joey one last look and turned to face them. There were half a dozen of them, three with knives out in their hands. I heard Louis's feet shuffling out of the way. He wouldn't want to get caught in the middle.

The three with knives rushed, then stopped short and began moving in slowly, circling, remembering their training. The rest were behind them, waiting. One of the three with knives had circled till I could see him only with the corner of my eye. The other two held still. I was well boxed, but I waited for the one behind to make a feint. And he did, toward the side of my head and I managed to hold it still and reach for him under the knife arm. I caught hold of his jacket and swung him hard, back into the other two. It threw the three of them off balance. But that was all—I'd had no heart for it. There was a yell from the back and the whole gang rushed me.

They were just kids. I couldn't put my heart in it. I couldn't kick them in the stomach. I couldn't fight through them. I could only try to hold them off for a while. To what end, I didn't know. I retreated slowly toward the table and they came after me.

And then I heard him—yelling at them, his voice high and cracking a little, and the rush stopped. I looked up and he was standing on the table, yelling at them.

"Leave him alone!" he yelled. "Knock it off!"

They gaped at him.

"You guys go on home," he said.

There was a wail from the crowd. A voice said:

"Joey! What about Stella?"

"We ain't going," Joey said. "You heard me. Go on home."

Somebody started swearing loudly.

"Shut up!" Joey said. "Get on home."

I started to walk away along the table, back toward the partition and the stairs. I had another slow, delayed reaction. That click in the loudspeaker. The sudden silence from the other end. It was no good. It was no good at all. I started to run. I heard Joey's voice.

"Wait!"

I had one foot on the step when I looked back. He was running toward me.

"Wait! About Stella—"

"Come on then," I said.

I got up the steps fast and he came along. I ploughed through the bedroom into the kitchen and the sentry I'd knocked out was trying to get on his feet. I went past him into the alley and Joey's feet pounded behind me.

"This way," I said and we got to the Buick.

I got the door open on the wheel side and slid in. Joey yanked the back door open and climbed in there. As I pulled away, unable to pass the truck, backing to the next street, he scrambled over the back of the seat into the front.

I swung crazily into the street, then pushed it hard, paying no attention to the signals. It was a short drive. When I pulled up in front of Beasly's garage, the motor was still trying to get warmed up.

I piled out, heard Joey coming, and got into the garage. The service department was deserted. The mechanics had knocked off for the night. The double doors stood open to the rental department. I ran through there, vaulted over the counter toward the little office in the back. I started to push through the door, then stopped, putting my hand up to stop Joey.

Herman Beasly was lying across his desk, the microphone still clutched in one pudgy hand. There was a widening circle of blood under his right temple.

Joey gulped. I pulled him back out to the street at a run. We got in the car again and I twisted it in a U-turn and headed down the long, dark street.

CHAPTER TWENTY-FIVE

There was a big black car parked in front of the apartment. The old quiet street had gone to sleep for the night. I got out of the Buick and ran up the walk. Joey's feet pounded after me through the front door and up the long stairs. It was dark and he stumbled once and picked himself up. I couldn't wait for him.

As I made the last turn at the top of the steps, I heard her voice, high and queenly out of the closed studio. I paused for a moment, so glad to hear it that the shock stunned me. Then I got to the door and found it locked. I stepped back, stumbling over Joey's feet, gave myself a push from the opposite wall and hit the door. It smashed and I fell all the way through it onto the floor.

I heard her scream once, then the gun, once, twice, three times. I was on my hands and knees and I pushed up and got so I could see something.

I saw her, leaning against the closed bedroom door with the gun in her hand, her arms and legs slack like a puppet's so that she seemed about to slide down to the floor. Sprawled at her feet was a small, delicate man with white hair, a twisted *pince-nez* sticking out from under his cheek. His thin, almost effeminate hands were flat on the floor, the fingers of one stretched toward a little blue automatic. But he was stone-cold dead and could no longer make use of it.

I led the Duchess out of the narrow hall, past him, into the studio. She stared at the gun for a long time, then handed it to me. I put it away, made her sit down.

"He came in—" she said dully, "with that gun—he wanted the girl—he threatened—"

"You had to do it," I said, "and I'm sorry."

I don't think she heard me.

"He did it," she said, "didn't he? Arline and Bill."

"And another, that you'll never have to see, a ward heeler named Beasly, who no doubt tried to shake him down."

"I thought I knew it—about Arline and Bill, but I didn't think he'd come here. I guess he flipped. He should have known better than to lie to me about having sat by the telephone all that evening. I tried to call him and got no answer. Then there was the blouse—" She stared at me.

Joey, gazing at the walls of the studio, said, "This place—I been here —" The Duchess looked at him blankly, then at the thin figure of her husband sprawled on the floor.

"He must actually have worn it when he did it—both times. It was yours, in that house—it would be available to him. I don't know whether he did it to throw suspicion on you. There could be other reasons—psychological reasons that would fit. He was a little effeminate, he wasn't at home in the world, nor with you, nor with himself. Violence could come out of it. I don't know."

Her voice was low and distant.

"Why? Why, Mac?"

"Bill was about to blow the whistle on him, on the Mr. Smith angle. He used the kid gangs for cover. They were stealing for him. It didn't really make sense till I heard how much was involved, and when I saw how it could be organized, with all those fancy trappings that only a man like him could handle really.

"But even all that, I think, was incidental. It was because Bill belonged to you, got love from you in a way he never could, maybe didn't even know he wanted. And the little girl belonged to you, too, even though he'd managed to take her away.

"But you know all this better than I do."

"I know," she said. "I guess he knew everything I did, every move. He must always have known about this place—" The bedroom door opened. Light fell on the man on the floor. Stella looked down, caught her breath and leaned against the jamb, staring. Joey moved toward the hall, looking at her, then stopped at the dead man's feet.

"That's—" he said, "that's Mr. Cameron!"

"That's Mr. Smith, Joey," I said.

He looked at me, then down the hall toward Stella.

"You O.K., Stella?" he said.

She was peering, trying to find him.

"Joey—?"

"Yeah, Stella."

"Go ahead, Joey," I said. "You can make it."

He felt his way along the hall, stepping carefully, looking down as he went. He got to the door and Stella put out a hand. Joey went into the room with her. I heard her crying.

The Duchess sat stiffly in the chair with her hands in her lap. I put my own over them. Mine were dirty and bloodstained and hers were clean and white and cold. I felt them relax, grow warmer, as I held them. Little by little she relaxed all over. The stiffness went away.

171

We stayed like that a long time. After a while she cried some, but quietly, so that I didn't notice it till later when I found my shoulder damp. She wasn't crying when she raised her head finally and looked around the room.

"What now, Mac?" she said.

"We'll be all right," I said, "after a little sleep."

Her arms curled around my neck.

"Then sleep now, Mac, right here."

"It's the best invitation I ever had," I said, "but there are some telephone calls to be made."

She let me go then and I found my way to the phone.

"What about Joey?" she said.

"He'll be all right, too," I said, "thanks to Joe DiMaggio."

I found I was dialing the number of Dr. Morton Stein.

www.ingramcontent.com/pod-product-compliance
Lightning Source LLC
Chambersburg PA
CBHW020643180626
46816CB00003B/1099